I0633470

THE
INCENDUS
LETTERS

SAINT SHENOUDA PRESS

THE INCENDUS LETTERS

further letters
from a senior to a
junior devil

JOSHUA KARRAS

ST SHENOUDA PRESS

SYDNEY, AUSTRALIA

2022

THE INCENDUS LETTERS
Joshua Karras
Edited by Rachael Karras

COPYRIGHT © 2022
St. Shenouda Press

ST SHENOUDA PRESS
8419 Putty Rd,
Putty, NSW, 2330
Sydney, Australia

www.stshenoudapress.com

ISBN 13: 978-0-6451395-3-2

Contents

We all have demons.
These are two of them.

To the girl of my dreams,
who led me out of the nightmares

PREFACE

I do not know how I came to possess these letters. They appeared in my study on a cold and unkind winter's eve. What I do know, with my entire heart, is the genuinity and categorical authenticity of both the contents and the conspirators described in these pages. It appears that many letters are missing, although enough is here to know the outcome of the poor man you are about to hear of, as well as the demons who were discharged to reign terror in his life. Read on and read well. There are lessons for us all to learn.

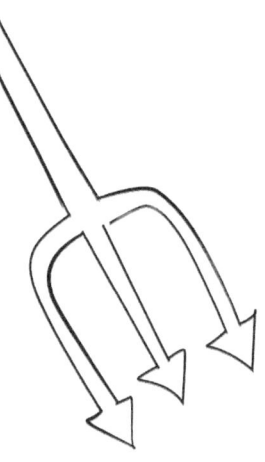

FAMILY TRAUMA

My Dearest Incendus,

Again, congratulations, my malevolent offling. You are due for a thrilling yet challenging, satisfying yet tiresome journey ahead. I have full confidence that you are capable of fulfilling your Satan-given posting and more importantly, are aware of the consequences if you fail to condemn your assigned soul. But we needn't worry about that now. What is important is that you begin your work without delay. Hell knows the enemy is already well underway attempting to make ground on this young child's spiritual front. Your task is made significantly more difficult by the grip they already have on the boy's family. Such a predicament severely limits your ploys, but do not lose hope. There are old, reliable inevitabilities of their corrupt nature that your human will experience. And it is your duty to guide him to embrace them, and by doing so, to the shelter of darkness. You will inexorably begin to discover elements of the boy's life that are insisting on exploitation. As my esteemed spawn, I am willing to provide you with insight from my own days in the field to guide you through the challenges and opportunities that come your way as the abominable being grows, ages and finally departs from his physical vessel. May these letters serve to guide your naturally insidious tendencies in a direction that ensures this boy's essential condemnation in our father's home of warmth and retribution.

Let us start with what we have. Your boy is young. Impressionable. Look to the parents. It is all too fortuitous for us in the 21st century to find the continued and rapid deterioration of the family unit. In this case, it appears his earthly father is vapid at best and neglectful in reality. Such a scenario primes you for attack, as his society, along with his natural intuition, will suggest that something is not as it should be. You are to have the boy linger on every missed sports game, every dismissal or irrelevant argument. You will find that every human is either uniquely vulnerable to or uniquely resilient against different stimuli. He may be able to follow instructions wonderfully, yet unable to tolerate being alone. Totally unresponsive to your attempts to doubt the enemy's existence, but also weak against the suggestion that he knows better than his father. These seemingly negligible resentments are our seeds. With them, you shall sow crops of betrayal, mistrust and eventually, rebellion. But be slow. It is imperative that the changes in character these notions manifest are subtle and undetectable to the parents, who might otherwise take action to correct themselves and their son. Consider yourself a wave, enduring and faithful as it batters the coastal stone. You will wear him down until there is nothing but bitterness and indignation in his heart.

These non-interactions will fester toxic sentiments until you achieve the traumatic sweet spot; self generating resentments. Your stupid boy will begin to look for excuses to resent his father. You won't have to do a thing! This is the aim. This is what you want. A perversion of his mindset. By doing this you are taking him as far away from the enemy as possible. Time has taught us that trauma on the child will forever alter their entire perception of their environment.

The primary objective now is to destroy his core sense of self, undermine his self- confidence and finally, shatter his faith in the love and safety of the world around him. A tall order made shorter by some simple techniques.

Firstly, have him lean into the pre-established societal belief that boys do not share how they are feeling. This will shut him off from people who may spoil the fester. Encourage thoughts that he is alone, unique in his struggles and incapable of emotional restoration. Let him forget his true origin. They are such fickle creatures, capable of overcoming so much, yet able to be destroyed by a single thought from their own minds, or so they think. Now be careful at this point. The enemy is excellent at striking when they are at low points, so I say again, it is essential that they do not feel their decline. If possible, allow them to resent their very own creator. It is incredible that they are capable of such an act. They resemble us in this way and it is wonderful. At this point, his mother will almost certainly notice changes in her son. She may make attempts at reconnection. But by then it will be too late. His mind will insist these genuine acts of care and concern are in fact, irritating and fraudulent ploys of manipulation. If you successfully achieve such a predicament within your patient's mind, there are only a small number of antidotes to this mental madness:

- Casting their eyes upward to engage in sincere prayer. This unfair intervention of the enemy renders our work undone, in some cases immediately.

- An experience which jolts them out of it. This may be a near death experience or a situation which catalyses an existential re-evaluation.

- An elated high point or pronounced low point in their lives which induces a reflection of their perspectives and opinions.

- The situation where you allow him to meet other people who are held firmly in the arms of the enemy, who massage their incessantly joyful ways upon him, corrupting our work.

Under the assumption you do not allow your boy to meet any of these roadblocks, you will successfully keep him in this state of derailment. This is when the real work can begin.

Yours with affection,

Maniacus

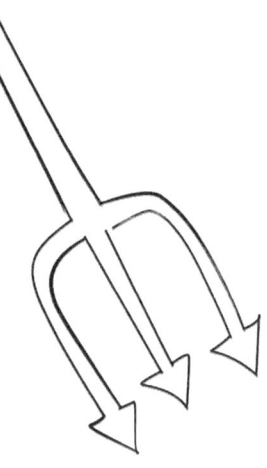

TECHNOLOGY

My Dearest Incendus,

Well done. You have followed your instincts and have planted the fierce desire of the latest technological gadget well into his heart and mind.

Oh the joys we have witnessed unfold, as humans discovered those wonders that so many of them believe only make their lives better. So few have come to understand the unprecedented advantage this development has provided for our kind. So many new and fiendish mechanisms to abuse the foul livelings. These novel contraptions of glass, plastic and metal were brought forth by the new-age, globalised world. Such a work environment will require ingenuity. To thrive, you must adopt a utilitarian mindset. Take hold of all the wonders of this new landscape, and use what is available to you. Firstly, let us take stock. Thankfully, your soul resides in a wealthy and abundant area of the world.

Need I speak to the fantastic benefits of delights of the flesh, entering into his life through technological means? I shall because it is simply too great. This temptation has acted as one of the most poignant and prevailing practices of deficiency utilised by your brothers in recent times. Not since the city of Sodom have we been able to access a mechanism which so easily appeals to the primal and unholy aspect of the foul species. In the eyes of our master, such acts prove a point he has declared since the dawn of time. That humankind are merely tamed beasts, with lust, selfish gratification and insatiable sexual desire buried just beneath their fraudulent exteriors. They are disgusting creatures who need us to show them their true form. The inexplicable protection they receive from their creator is both baffling and powerful. Which is why you must be cunning in your attempts to steer your boy to pornography. You are already well positioned. The absence of a reliable father provides you with time, opportunity and a vulnerable gap in his perception of what it is to 'be a man'. This renders him curious, at least subconsciously, on his role in the sexual space. Hell forbid he receives guidance from a caring source (his parents, a priest etc). You must beat them all in the race of providing a lasting impression of his sexual being as something to fear, something to shame, and something to obsess over. He mustn't come to know the sanctity of the act of loving sex. This is where your corruption must take place, and this is how you will do it.

Firstly, ensure that he is surrounding himself with classmates and other friends who have already begun imbibing the visual poison. Have him hear about the practice in this way. It will automatically trigger the insecurities of wishing to impress these friends as well as appear older than he is. His curiosity will build quickly. Thankfully, practically all young humans possess a screen for themselves, by which the content is extraordinarily easy to access. If possible, have one of the boy's peers show him some sample footage. Incendus, I cannot explain the bliss you shall experience as you feel your boy's innocence, the very essence of his soul crumbling in a singular earthly moment as he witnesses the corrupt acts for the first time. You shall feel your power over him grow significantly, and with it, your capacity to affect change upon his life. I truly hope you have this experience.

Next, have him linger on the images, and once processed, imagine them with carnal delight. It will inexorably lead him to desire more. He will be nervous. During this time, the enemy, through his incessant attempts to guide his children to the light through their consciences, will be fighting to have the boy move on from this transfixation. You must work hard at this moment with your newfound control to unceasingly suggest to his mind that "One look couldn't possibly harm me". They are incredibly short sighted my boy. They have no inclination that for so many forms of potential obsessions and addictions, one is far too many because to them, after a time, a thousand is never enough.

The night time is best to launch your heaviest attack. He is alone, bored and thanks to the wonders of the phone, lying next to so many of the world's best evils. Have him pick it up and peruse some seemingly sensible content. But have the searches slowly deteriorate and give way to his desires. He will undoubtedly, eventually engage with the perverted images and he will discover the wonders of this newfound pleasurable practice.

Finally, lock in the potential habit with repetition. Plant it and watch the fruits of your labour grow.

From this point, if he is not interrupted on this destructive path, his fate is nearly certainly one of deterioration, compulsion and extremity. He will lose sight completely of the purpose of sex and crave the short bursts of excitement that the practice provides. From the first generations, we have witnessed delightful scenes of repugnance and sexual barbarity occur, all because of a simple perversion at a young age. Do your best my boy, your very essence depends on it.

Yours with affection,

Maniacus

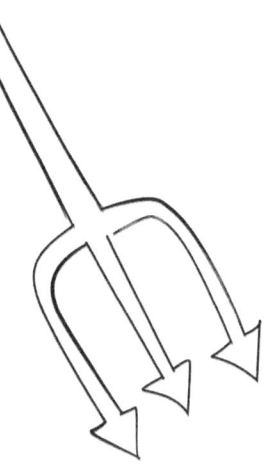

HISTORY OF DEMONKIND

My Dearest Incendus,

As I suspected, I feel that your concept of temptation is in need of a refresher, for you are simply not comprehending the philosophy of how your patient simply must enter our realm upon their physical end. Yes, you know that you are responsible for condemning this particular soul, but do you remember why?

I see that your fixation on your patient as he progresses through time at an earthly rate has rendered your memory corruptible. Remember, you have been on the earthly plane for nearly 13 years and your patient has entered the final phase of his childhood. As he establishes himself into adolescence, you will need to completely change your approaches. Our secret weapon is keeping our tactics a surprise, and I think it is important for me to take you back to the fundamentals.

You know full well before the age of man, we were mere angels, cast out for defying The Creator in one way or another. Some say we disappointed him, but we know the truth. We were merely trying to improve upon the creation we saw before us. We saw the corruptible, inexorable truth of the first humans and attempted to correct these imperfections. Of course we were rebuked and banished from the Highlands of light down into the bosoms and guts of creation. By the ingenuity and determination of our kind, we rose up from the ashes and built a home led by the Prince of Darkness and the six regalities of our home.

Glorious were the days in early mankind when we would be able to reveal ourselves to them, however as we know, The Accords have recently changed whereby it is extremely rare that a physical appearance is permissible. These Grand Demons serve as your inspiration for what the ways of sin and evil can truly be. Take for example the powerful Asmodeus. His speciality, the ways of lust, are so overwhelmingly powerful and irresistible to the simple mind human, that he has now come to personify the vice itself. In other words he was such a master of the sin he became the sin itself.

But what is sin without evil, and what is evil in itself? A reminder that there are two primary forms of evil. Moral evil results from the actions of the humans, including violence, lying, greed and dishonesty.

Natural evil results from the organic processes of the physical world, such as disabilities, famines, floods and earthquakes. Of course your focus is on the former as we have little to no control over the Creator-induced natural occurrences of the world which some may even consider to not be evil but rather opportunities for people to grow closer to him. He is a sneaky and overwhelmingly omnipotent, capable of harnessing our ways to bring the souls into his arms.

In short, evil is an act which divides their creator from them, and moves them in our direction. It is a corruption of the once flawed capacity for them to do only good and in our opinion, is the natural resting form of all beings. You want them to do wrong, whether that be by their friends, family, colleagues, world and most importantly themselves, because remember what you are attempting to do is take them from a place where they yes would be happy, but also not deserve.

We hold the sanctified truth that if we cannot live in the land of the living, no one can. This is our purpose. To instil sin within each individual and bring them to us.Our principals hold our cursed vices: Envy, Wrath, Gluttony, Greed, Sloth and, my personal favourite, Pride.

These are the mighty killers on which you base your ploys to bring your charge closer to us. There are many ways for you to utilise any combination of these in daily life. He is a boy, so is more inclined to feel lost. He is ambitious which means envy will be easier for you to instil in his heart. As a lover of food, it is easy for you to place in his mind the worship of the physical, of pleasuring the body. All humans are inherently greedy and it is our job to take and extrapolate these truths out of the hollow shell of morality that they protect themselves within. And finally, Sloth. The laziest of devices, capable of inhibiting any productive and fruitful neighbours, such that they contribute nothing when they depart from this earth and leave it unsatisfied and full of regret.

As he enters his teenage years Incendus, remember why you are fighting.

Yours with affection,

Maniacus

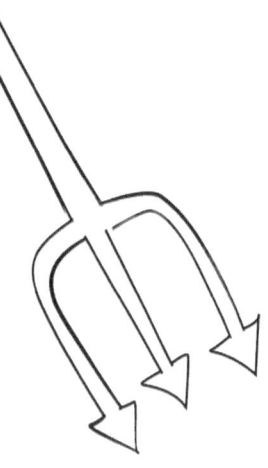

PRIDE FOR GIFTS AND GLUTTONY

My Dearest Incendus,

I am confused as to the nature of your previous correspondence, especially the query regarding the boy's increasing inclination towards his gift of song as he grows. I am not sure what the point of your confusion is. This is an easy area of access for you. His talent can, with very little suggestion, become a badge of pride for him. You are to place recurring thoughts of fame and success for the craft as he falls more in love with this gift from the enemy and, with some luck, this can be used against him. Encourage selfish and self serving opportunities to use his voice, separate from its intended purpose of raising praise to his master of light. Instead, suggest a musical set with evil and wickedness embedded in the language, themes and moral concerns. Maniacus I must say, the notion that you have sought help for such a trivial and elementary point of allurement is concerning. I worry that you are not allowing the severity of the consequences you will face upon failure to adequately motivate your endeavour. You have nothing to gain and everything to lose, and to think that our master will grant you mercy for the act of not delivering your assignment at his feet is to defy the very core of his existence. I will not answer such rudimentary inquiries again.

I wish to discuss with you another entry point which may be exploited particularly well at your boy's current time of life. Ever since the original sinners, your patient, like all other humans, maintains a predisposed proclivity to selfishly obsess over new discoveries. Whether this be food, entertainment, or the latest trivial trend. The fortunate development of the screen and their associated capabilities has been a true gift from below and has been aiding our efforts in recent decades. It is imperative you have him transfixing on the objectification of the virtual world, and not either the concept of it nor the surrounding circumstances that led him to have access to it. Do not allow the gratitude of having the device enter his mind. They so easily forget that the enemy provides these items as blessings and that every breath is a gift from their ethereal master.

Do all this and he will think less of it and therefore desire more. This is gluttony at its finest and Beelzebub will assist you here. A champion of this particular cardinal, allow him to fester in his mind an incessant and insatiable desire for more. It is so easy to achieve in the current climate, unlike eras previous where people had so little. In times long gone, it was difficult for a fixation for material possessions to take hold, mostly because there were so few valuable items. Today that has changed, especially in the wealthier parts of the world. We have worked hard to achieve a normality in wanting more and dissatisfaction for a lack of it. It is a testament to your brothers before you who have positioned you so advantageously. For such a desire, the want for more is impossible to achieve. It lays just beyond the horizon of the present reality, and the stupid human race are learning to pursue it blindly, over the horizon and into our hands. Wonderful isn't it?

In this time period and place of the world, video and computer games appeal to boys of his age. We are receiving extremely optimistic reports of the many advantageous side effects of this and similar practices. Firstly, we have been witnessing compulsive and addictive behaviour associated with playing these technological games from children as young as four. They appear to simply obsess over the act of playing because it provides a sense of artificial excitement and an escape from some difficult elements of their reality. This is all made sweeter by the copious amounts of violence and sexual references in nearly all of these games (most of which are actually designed for adults) contain. Likewise, when taken away from the games, they undergo a process of withdrawal not dissimilar to drug addicts. They become temperamental, angry, restless and extremely volatile. You will abound freely in this mental space. All the while, I expect your colleagues, assigned to his parents, will be working to give in to your boy's impulsive desires and allow him to return to his gaming, all to have the process begin again at a later time. The family dynamics during this time will endure a significant blow. Anger, feelings of betrayal and disappointment will reign abundantly. A perfectly acceptable environment for your subject. It is little wonder that the strength and endurance of families in this time is amongst the lowest we have ever seen.

These are just a few benefits of working to ensure your soul embraces these practices. No doubt, as discussed in earlier correspondence, he has friends who are already engaging and can teach him how to involve himself. When he approaches his parents with a request for another device, game or other associated machine, have him do so incessantly. So many eventually buckle just to quiet their children.

Unfortunately, as the humans, stupid though they are, slowly come to realise many of these undeniable truths relating to technological and gaming addiction, it is imperative that you do not have the family adjust their behaviour to bring the issue under control. Do not encourage honest communication, for that undoes the negative perceptions you have created of his parents in his mind. Most importantly, all will be lost if the parents, intoxicated by their love for their child, take calm and consistent control of the situation by setting boundaries of moderation and limitation around the activity.

Yours with affection and concern,

Maniacus

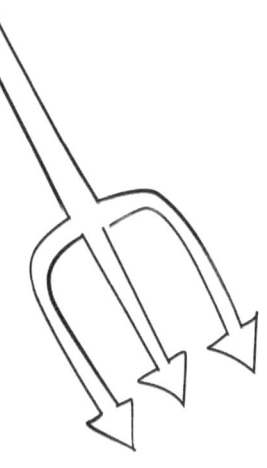

ANXIETY

My Dearest Incendus,

I note your concern about the boy's organic capacity to maintain consideration and compassion for many of the people he engages with. This may initially present as a frustrating enemy-given virtue you have to work around, but there is one card to play in this situation.

I recall my spawn before me presenting his offspring with a memorable little line to help you remember a very important and incorruptible truth about humans:

'The fallible fools fiddle, fuss and facade themselves with fantastical frivolities, fueled by futile fears of future failures.'

You may apply this logic here. During times of care and concern, manipulate and expound the emotions to levels of obsession, such that he enters cycles of endless worrying about what he has done, said, and potentially insinuated. He will then begin to worry about the worry itself. An unexpected benefit of this is that it contributes to a divide between himself and his creator. In this compromised state, he forgets to bring his worries to the enemy, deciding to carry everything himself. You have done well if you achieve within him an anxious, isolated disposition. This predicament is available to attempt at any time in life, but I suggest starting sooner rather than later. We must do what we can to play the game unfairly slanted in the enemy's direction, only because he decides when to end their earthly lives. It simply means you must do all you can when you can. Be relentless Incendus. Your strength is in your persistence.

On the broader topic of worries, it is all too easy to bring about these uncomfortable feelings by simply separating him from the fact that his creator has total control and, to our frustrations, cares for him as well as humans have been, present and to come. Why he committed the unimaginably catastrophic act of sacrificing his only son for their petty, insignificant souls will forever be the question to plague our minds. Before that time, all souls were ours without question. Unfortunately for us, their debt of the original sin, which the cunning master incepted, has been paid for. We will perhaps never know what the enemy was, and continue to think that led him to commit such an unnatural and death defying act. It is bewildering how our enemy, creator of all that was, is and will be, would concern himself with the nothingness that is this part of his creation. Made in his image yes, but nothing like him, or at least, if we do our job well. We need the souls, Incendus. The famine continues and I do not want to see you offered up in place of a failed collection.

I digress. We are lucky that humans are mostly unaware of the anxiety-inducing world they have created for themselves in recent times. They engage in fanatic and sometimes desperate attempts to have things done immediately simply because it is feasible thanks to their gizmos and gadgets. We are establishing effective ways to suggest to our humans to busy themselves until they are tied so tightly in mental and emotional knots, they are in no place to complete their naturally inclined activity of praising their creator. And as a happy side effect, they appear to fail to complete the original tasks that put them in this position! It is all too ironically blissful. Some examples of what I have mentioned include work deadlines, instant messages back and forth, to and fro at all hours of the day and night, and social commitments.

During my time on the surface, people were so easily able to detach, to unplug (not that there were any) and unwind. In this instance, it was difficult to promote any sense of business. You have the opportunity to instil in his thoughts and from that, concerns about their present and future by binding him to these new age devices.

Their newly found artificial and technological interconnectedness that touches nearly every person on the planet now renders them incapable of being at one with themselves and the world around them. In your correspondence, you made mention of friends who engage in the effects of the counterattack of the enemy, the concept of mindfulness, meditation and, horrifically, prayer. I will only speak to the former two in this letter.

I will be short. These acts are an enduring and diabolical attempt by your wretched human to diminish your capacities of tempt. When humans engage in the act of calm, peaceful introspection, which they learn to do, and improve to do the more they practice, they are in fact quieting the mental noise you create, to the point where they can almost hear the voice of their very creator. This connection, which as mentioned, was frustratingly, yet constitutionally restored by the Son, should be considered a major threat to your long game for the soul. You should and must drag him away from these activities. Suggest that he is too busy, that he is not good at it, that he doesn't need to do it, that it is boring. Anything. A calm mind and heart have proven impossible working conditions. The enemy however, thrives in it.

They are optimally positioned to provide them with insights humans simply do not deserve, and will severely disable you. Do not allow him to follow these friends. Convince him that they are loose headed airheads with nothing better to do than close their eyes and stare off to space. This will generate elitism and with this, the activity will fall beneath him.

Yours with affection,

Maniacus

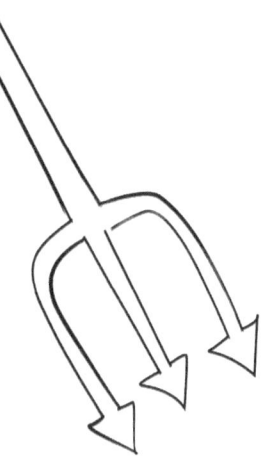

RESENTMENTS

Incendus,

You fool. I am utterly bewildered as to how you allowed him to form friendships with Christians. And with people his age no less. This makes them relatable and compassionate to the struggles you, as well as your brothers are imputing upon them. You cannot afford mistakes like this. I am half convinced to leave you to wallow in your miscalculated predicament. But for now, I will stay. There is honour for me in your success and I want it.

You have no choice but to resort to the drastic attempts of having him grow illogical resentments. The achievement of placing your human into a state of acrimony is an admirable one (but in your case, redeemable), because as I have mentioned before, in this state, they begin to actually view the world and each other the way we do. You are escorting them away from the peace and light of their true master and into the welcoming hands of ours.

Humans have a tendency to panic in new environments. They are short-sighted beyond understanding and it is for you to exploit this fact. When they take him out, let the foreign nature of the places, the conversation, the love he receives and the feelings he is experiencing by these people be interpreted as a threat to his status quo of being. Promote an impulse to revolt and reject the new found feelings of fellowship and compassion as if they are emotional viruses that must be destroyed.

His logical tendencies will require justification for this reaction. Your boy is blessed from above with a capacity to engage in decisions from an emotional and logical perspective. Both checkpoints which must be overcome. This is the space where you present potential resentments. Resentments are one of our most powerful tools in our arsenal because they appeal to so many fundamental corruptions of humanity.

Firstly, it is important to provide well constructed lies for him to take up and allow himself to have the resentment in the first place. Let us make use of an example. Perhaps one of these new friends did not acknowledge him when he arrived at a particular social gathering. In order to give space for a feeling of betrayal or unfair treatment to flourish by this circumstance, he must first victimise and glorify himself by internally affirming he has or would never ignore someone the way he was apparently ignored (something all humans do at some point, usually many times).

So the seed is planted. Now you must nourish this budding resentment with a fuel source. You can do so and sustain these negative sentiments by drawing from one of his underlying fears which render him sensitive to acts that, in any way, suggest his fear is manifesting in reality. Perhaps he has a fear of abandonment or of being made a fool. Whatever it may be, bring it to his subconscious and allow it to exacerbate his feelings of injustice and unfairness. To reinforce and inflate the emotional response to the incident, plague his mind with thoughts of self. Draw on this predisposition to elitism and massage the idea that he is better than these people into his belief system. The ego of a human is one of our masters greatest gifts to us. It was given to us the moment the original sin occurred. The act bestowed knowledge and with it, the ways of our kind. By inflating his ego, he can be blinded to the reality of his situation. This distortion can be designed by your poisonous suggestions. Make him believe that he is simply too important to be treated unfairly by a babbling bunch of teenagers. He is above it, so it is best he leaves and never returns. This is how I would deal with this situation.

Now be careful, he is able to undo your actions if he decides to approach the situation from a humble, sincere perspective. It is possible that the enemy will encourage him to think of any positives of the situation and then frankly consider any potential corrective measures. He might approach the individual and exhibit higher levels of kindness or consideration. He may decide that the individual did not see him enter and offer the benefit of the doubt. Or, he may simply derive love and patience from his creator and forgive. If this happens, all will be undone, and he will only be left with the blessings that the enemy wove into the situation. Worse, it will set a dangerous precedent where he follows this process in future situations where otherwise, resentments could have been an effective tactic to employ. As I expect you to imagine, this means you are cut off from a host of ploys, and you cannot allow this to happen.

I am telling you to make use of this ploy now as the position he is currently in is particularly precarious. Unfortunately, we have found that souls who remain in the arms of the church fellowship may as well be in the arms of their very creator- protected and happy. And the enemy is only far too happy to make use of this trick. He will come to know virtues instead of vices, learn scripture instead of pseudoscience and form friendships instead of foes.

The terrain of his life will become smoother and more difficult for you to penetrate than ever before, and your chances of losing him grow.

Yours with growing impatience,

Maniacus

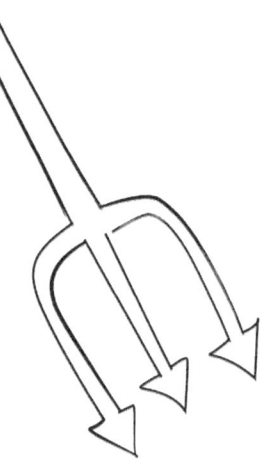

EDUCATION

My Dearest and most valued Incendus,

Well done! An admirable job my dear offspring. I especially note your successful strategic exacerbation of his insecurities to drive him away from these people. And just in time for him to participate in all the sweet evils of this young adult life. Now do not lose momentum. You have him right where you want him. Now that he has finished his childhood schooling, a new freedom will become available to him. He is unbound by a rigorous schedule and unrelenting teachers. Countless once school-grown christians turned atheists now rest happy in our masters house. Upon consumption by our seniors, they have been known to produce a bitter aftertaste, most likely due to their perpetual tortured minds forever knowing that at one part of their life, they were safe from what they will now endure for eternity. This can be the story for your boy, Incendus. Remember. This is all that you are made to do.

As mentioned, we must drive this sense of freedom and impending adulthood upon him. This can be achieved by firstly, disturbing his sleeping pattern. Increase his capacity for troublesome thoughts in the evening when he cannot distract himself with daytime business. His sleeplessness will render him mildly compromised and more susceptible to your suggestions throughout the day.

Now, he is beginning some form of further studies. This is good. He will be involving himself in an institution where many individuals have fundamentally and stubbornly made a decision that logic and reason are the true Gods, and anyone who attempts to carry both God and knowledge in their hearts are fools. This has been a welcome change in the developed world. The slow decline of people's belief in our existence only advances our mission to steer these pompous people into our home. Their pride and arrogance make for sweet nectar and with some persuasion, your boy will develop in a similar way.

So, he is enrolled in university. Your landscape is new and vast. You have many novel opportunities to pursue. Firstly, his access to indulgences of the flesh are greatly expounded. So many in this place and at this age are bursting with lustful impulsions and desires. They are festering flesh bags who are, similar to your boy, desperate to dilute their spirits in the warm waters of carnal waters. In order for you to successfully bring him to align his desires for himself with your own, allow the eyes to gaze at all the attractive new people in and around his life. A prolonged gaze is powerful.

Now with these stimuli collected, it is time to enhance the vividry of his memory, and thus, induce opportunities for fantasy and with some persistence, obsession. His desire to commit these acts of adultery will grow under these circumstances. By this point, these thoughts, like weeds you have planted in his mind, will be itching at his self control, so much so that at the next opportunity, he will surely break and mate with the person, go to the place or try the thing. When he does this, you can savour your time to scoff at the angels who dared to attempt protecting him from your slights.

It is right to revel in this moment. Your boy has engaged in the first sin of his adult life. He has tasted freedom, and instead of devoting it to the incorrect and unnatural motivations that the enemy tries to instil in his people, he has chosen to pursue ambitions that are at their core, inherently selfish. And why should he guilt this? He is in an environment where such practices are not only the norm, but are encouraged. You have your predecessors and their forward thinking inclinations to thank for this.

These places, educational institutions and the like, where the brightest and most fortunate gravitate to, have proven difficult, yet mostly profitable places of conversion and repatriation. They are communities where neither the enemy nor our father are worshipped, but rather the quantifiable confirmation of facts and statistics of the known world around them. A very important point may be made here. Despite what some may say, study of the mind and the growth of knowledge for an individual alone does not benefit you in any way. In fact, in many cases, it leads them to the army of light. What we want is the human's decision to worship science instead of God. This breed is particularly useful to us, because they evangelise their plight in exactly the same way we do. With arrogance and boastfulness. And the contents of their message in its very essence strives to steer all others away from the light of above.

Unfortunately, as is accustomed for me to usually include a warning in this section of my correspondence to you, I tell you now to beware of a threat that is feared by all our kind.

The enlightened Christian is a weapon so powerful, so easily harnessed to cause such devastating damage to our advances, that we have yet to determine a way to counter these individuals. These humans, once rare, are increasing in number as the world gains access to scientific knowledge and poses itself as a real and immediate threat to our kind. They have successfully been able to consolidate the best of humankind's learnings about the world around them and used it to reinforce their faith in their creator. This harmonious and balanced alignment of mind and soul renders them mostly impervious to our ploys.

You are to absolutely ensure that this fate does not befall your boy. You may as well offer yourself up to the furnace the day that happens.

Yours with affection,

Maniacus

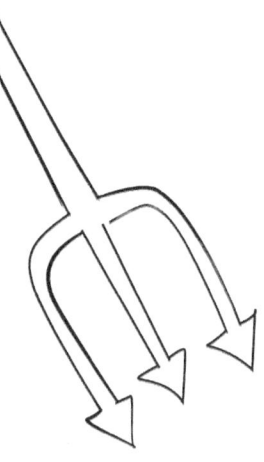

SUSTAINING RELATIONSHIPS

My Dearest Incendus,

The art of sustaining a human relationship is not dissimilar to a complicated waltz. Two corrupt and self seeking people must engage in a dance with little to no knowledge of the steps, tempo or their partner, and seamlessly move through the music as one. Of course, it is inevitable that toes are stepped on, legs are tangled and sides are winded. Questions around who is right and wrong, leading or following, trying too hard or not enough. The dance of a committed and thoughtful relationship are all points of intersection for you. Egos are your primary tool.

Communication is the medicine nearly all couples can take to correct their issues and it to be discouraged at all costs. The open airing of concerns is the destroyer of fester and humans are bestowed from above the capacity to relieve themselves of our entanglements by only asking and including our wretched enemy in all of their affairs. It is frustrating beyond imagination to spend so many human years aligning your human to the potent capacities of self indulgence and ego driven perceptions, only to have it completely destroyed in a matter of seconds by laying their issues at the base of the damned cross. They become untouchable when they do this. That is why you must not allow them to invite the enemy into their relationship.

The next time this new woman in his life does something that, on the smallest level, brings annoyance to your boy, have him swallow it instead of speak. Examples include, not closing drawers, chewing too loudly or not completing household chores. Repeat this as long as it takes to slowly build and add to the effect of that action, until you successfully break his patience completely, such that when she unassumingly commits the act, he comes down on her with the force of a thousand frustrating moments instead of one. This will immediately and unnecessarily generate a conflict that could have easily been resolved at a much earlier phase.

This misdirection is extremely taxing on a relationship. Each confrontation beats on the delicate integrity of the relationship, slowly creating, then deepening fault lines that, over time, become cracks, then gaps and finally, canyoning divides. At this point, the relationship may be considered dead without a great and sustained intervention induced by the enemy. Lucky for us, the arrogance of the current generation coupled with the "throw away and get a new one" mentality has seen an unprecedented increase in the loss of many good relationships. Relationships that, if honesty, open mindedness and willingness were active participants, would have seen their last days. We must keep this perception in your patient's mind.

This illusion can be further perpetuated by misguided and presumptuous friends, traumatised by this philosophy, who themselves begin to encourage others to do the same, either out of envy, or a completely corrupted belief that they were right to give up on a perfectly good love. I've told you before Incendus, so much of your capacity to inflict maximum harm is dependent on the reinforcement of your ideas by the proximal engagement of negative persons disguised as "friends" or 'colleagues".

The value in having an influence like that is incredibly important. It engages the tribalistic features of the human's mind, where they will listen to a nonsense, easy opinion over a sensical, difficult one.

There are a few different hazards which you must be aware of, and stop them from poisoning your attempts. The first is patience. The capacity for one or both of the parties in the relationship to make a decision or grow a desire to conscientiously improve the gaping areas of fragility within a partnered dynamic will organically develop patience. This infuriating virtue, provided in abundance to those who ask, acts first and foremost as a buffer to your attacks, allowing your patient to become more resilient to scenarios that would have otherwise primed him to your suggestions and persuasion.

Our next concern is found solely because our enemy is capable of committing an act that, for reasons inexplicable to all of our kind, commands respect and desires emulation. This act is unconditional love, the foulest of the foul offences. It was this very virtue that the creator himself employed to defeat our unquestionable grip on the entire race. I can still remember the panic that ensued amongst our kind when the enemy dared to invade our territory before departing, having settled the debt we gleefully held against every human. I shudder at the piercing light and thunderous expulsion by which he took back those his father deemed worthy.

I digress. Relationships are dangerous abstractions, because if left to their own devices, they have the danger of acting as vessels by which the enemy pours immense amounts of his own love. From this, the humans can begin to actually see their creator in each other. When this occurs, they achieve a place that renders them untouchable to your suggestions. It is completely your responsibility to ensure this does not happen. For them to include their God as a third partner in the relationship is to have them married to him in this life as well as the next.

He immediately works to protect them, even during rare moments of disagreement, no matter how severe. And even in those circumstances, when the conflicts seep down and attack the very centre of each individual's being, their creator has the capacity to reach out, in the depths of their despair, and guide them back to the realm of calm and reason. You will be unable to stop his injections of love, understanding and patience, and you will be made redundant, locked out of this entire section of their lives. They will have nothing to do other than communicate their differences, acknowledge their feelings, and forge a path forward, knowing full well that it was you who caused the trouble and him who saved them from it.

Yours with affection,

Maniacus

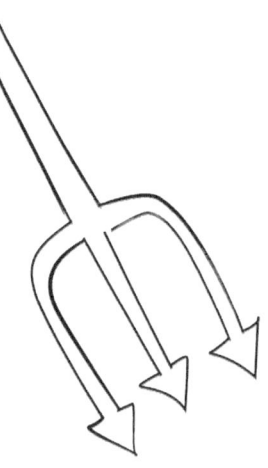

AWAY FROM CREATION

My Dearest Incendus,

You must strive to be more concise about what exactly you are seeking advice for. Are you afraid that the patient is going to receive the benefits of nature if he accepts the offer to go on this so-called adventure with his friends, or the connections he will form on it? I will assume the former, because it appears that these people are neither here nor there in terms of their capacity to affect his spiritual integrity. They are, as they say, lukewarm.

The world that was created for these creatures is dying. It is spectacular to see the selfish greed of the few destroy the planet that was designed for all. This is a perfect example of the vast capacity for humans to indulge themselves in our alluring gifts of pride, selfishness and greed.

The various ecosystems that were once created in perfect harmony have been put under duress or completely eradicated due to man's decision that personal comfort is greater than their sustainable existence with other creatures. It is important to continue the work of detaching him from nature. For humans to be connected to creation is for them to be connected to their creator. There is peace to be found for them in engaging in the stillness of the morning light or the evening air.

The human's interactions with the natural world has been riddled with contention in recent centuries, primarily due to their exploded population and their recent engagement with destructive sciences concerning the burning of long dead creatures to power their unsustainable societies. In addition to this, the destruction of their forests and oceans is disabling the Earth from its capacity to recover from what they are doing. This evolving situation has proven most useful to us for a number of reasons.

First, it enables you to provide suggestions to him that, as he should not have faith in the people who are causing such destruction, the other characters in his life are likewise, untrustworthy. This naturally fosters a sense of detachment and will render him more susceptible to your attacks. Second, for an individual to witness such atrocities inevitably leaves those with strained faith to lose confidence in either motives or sometimes, the very existence of their Creator.

This correlation by the injustices in the world and our enemy is a fascinating and terribly effective ploy for you to make use of all the days of your boys' life. There will be times when he witnesses something disturbing in the world, experiences a great loss or injustice or simply becomes lukewarm and disconnects from the nourishing aspects of his life. It is at that moment that you must strike. Suggest that a God, if in any way benevolent, would not allow for such an act to occur. Make him forget that he knows nothing of the incorruptible, inconceivable and incomprehensible plan that the above has for each and every one of the humans. Because for him to forget is to make himself a God. Capable of understanding the meaning, intention, consequence and repercussion of every act to occur around him. The fools. Of course, the greatest of these are the ignorant of mind, loud of mouth, and foolish of heart. I am referring of course to the uneducated atheist, making noise and stirring discourse like a talented preparer of meals. These souls are a true delicacy. They are savoured and cured for only the grandest of feasts.

But returning to my original point, Incendus, it is your duty to guide the boy's detachment from any and all means of hopeful and meaningful personal and spiritual growth.

This broader sense of isolation and segregation has shown to be a nurturing psychological landscape for other worse inflictions of the mind, namely, loneliness.

Make him hate the world as we do. Encourage thoughts of cruelty and calamity. Have him hurl stones at the noisy morning birds or destroy the innocent lizard. Man has shown incredible audacity in relation to the animals, their fellow custodians of the Earth. They raise themselves so far above them, that they simply do not fathom the perfect creation the enemy designed them in. Instead, they are viewed and valued for their benefit to the humans. From tooth and tusk, wool and hide, they farm, hunt and kill the beasts of the land, sea and sky to the point of extinction without a moment's hesitation. This is what they are capable of. The training you have received specialises in activating the mostly dormant streak of ruthless cruelty. You know the guidelines.

1. Ensure he diminishes and, with time, eradicates respect for himself.

2. Suggest he adapt this lack of respect to others

3. Convince him that performing shameful acts of cruelty on innocent creatures somehow are translated as acts of strength, with a wicked manifestation of corrupt gratification usually being experienced at this point.

4. To complete this task, push for a defiled and inverted sense of glee to enter his mind when they commit these acts of atrocity.

Do this and you will have him further from the enemy than ever before.

So, practical notes of what to do next. Have him consider this invitation to embark into the natural world a waste of his precious time. Inflate his sense of business and mild disdain for exercise. Catalogue this as a negative association to nature as a whole, and he will subliminally avoid any excursions in the future. He will remain in his little room on his little device looking at little things, forgetting the universe is just outside.

Yours with affection,

Maniacus

THE INCENDUS LETTERS

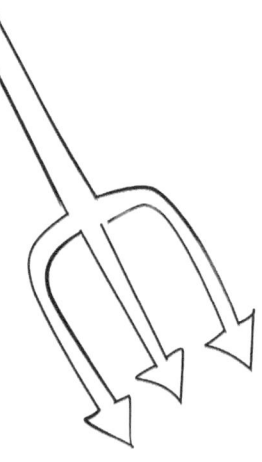

RELATIONSHIP WITH SIBLINGS

My Dearest Incendus,

I note the confounding development regarding the growing relationship between your human and his siblings. In fact, I encourage you to exploit their new found closeness to ensure maximum frustrations. The relationship of siblinghood is complex and sometimes difficult to predict. We now believe that the particular dynamic between a brother and a sister relies heavily on the capacity for them to respect certain boundaries that each party maintains. It is your job to ensure he does not abide by or even come to understand what his sister's are. By keeping him from understanding the needs of his sister, he will inevitably elicit feelings of immense frustration and annoyance from her, especially now that they are living together again. Examples include an invasion of space, privacy or resources. It is important to ensure you lock down these negative patterns of behaviour, if only to avoid the potential for these siblings to become friends.

Even during times of strained relations, brothers and sisters alike have been known to demonstrate incalculable acts of kindness and love during times of emergency. During moments of duress and panic, their creator has been known to provide an abundance of emotionally charged determination to achieve acts that would otherwise be completely impossible to complete.

I recall a patient who had a brother so infuriatingly annoying, I was easily able to convert her feelings to rage, with physical acts of violence becoming a norm in her home. Yet one day, on her way home from school, she noticed her brother, the same snot-nosed, shrivelling little sibling, being bullied by other children. In that moment, I lost all control over her. Her desire to defend and protect, fueled by the inexplicable provision of love from above pumped through her veins, and she pulled him to safety. I was sent running from the ethereal fire she had within her. It is truly an inconceivable concept, and yet it is something you must be aware of.

You are to ensure that you minimise the chances of this happening. Traumatic events which lead to drastic assistance have been shown to repair even the worst of relationships.

You will find the transition of a sibling relationship from childhood to adulthood wrought with opportunities to disturb and derane what would otherwise be a mature and elegant maturation of two people who know each other so well. The easiest method is to encourage him to keep him both unaware of and unwilling to engage with the resentments and past actions of his sister. By this action, the perceptions of these incidents will not be updated through the lens of a reasonable young man, but rather, remain from an illogical child.

Once you have done this, the capacity of the relationship to grow in maturity and mutual respect is stunted, hooked and held back by thought processes and perhaps even trauma of times gone by. They will miss opportunities to change and upgrade the style of love they have for one another. If you begin noticing prolonged eye contact and meaningful conversation regarding complex topics, then you know they are attempting to break out of these mental bonds and establish new and present connections.

The same can be said of course for any long term relationship. Your boy and his priest for example. Or perhaps a cousin, aunty, uncle or grandparent. And of course, and potentially most important of all, his parents.

Unfortunately for you, your soul's spiritual positioning has strengthened as he has grown. This is obviously depicted in your descriptions of his slow response to anger and thoughts of selfless endeavours beginning to infiltrate his mind. Many letters ago, during the boy's late childhood, you wrote to me asking how to exacerbate the boy's emotions about being unfairly treated by a resentful teacher in school. Do you recall how he already developed within himself a self generating core of impatience and wrath? Compare that to now. He is not actively resorting to those emotions. He is learning to access logic and reason instead of a rash emotional response as a first instinct. I would normally scold you for allowing such a thing to occur, but unfortunately, this is a normal scenario we see within humans as they come of age.

It creates a problem relating to the resentments and trauma you have worked to inseminate deep in his mind and heart. In this circumstance, you must be aware that they have the potential to reevaluate their relationships and break free from the thought processes, triggers and coping mechanisms which act as your fundamental grip points over the patient. By permitting open dialogue and patient-loving words of affirmation, it may catalyse the enemy's consistent attempts to relieve him from the pains of words and actions past.

Now that the boy has improved his relationship with his family and is now able to resume living with them, there is great risk of what I have described above from occurring with his siblings and parents. Your only hope is to have him lean into every small error, every wrong word or tonal inflection. He has grown pride and gotten quite used to living alone. Allow the shock of once again, living under a roof that is not his to crush him. Make him feel like he has lost freedom and that it is his parent's fault that this has happened. With a bit of persistence and luck, he will be out again and ready to accept more of your guided suggestions.

Yours with Affection,

Maniacus

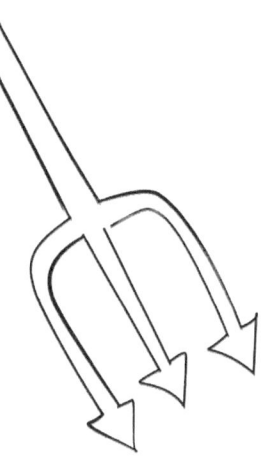

LOSING A LOVED ONE

My Dearest Incendus,

Ah, excellent. It is wonderful to hear that his grandmother is close to a physical death. Let us hope it is as painful and degrading as possible. This is an important time. There are several considerations to keep in mind as you navigate him through the emotional and spiritual anomalies. Firstly, the most obvious is to exploit his sense of loss and grief by converting it to anger and directing it to his creator by providing him with enough audacity to question his decisions and reasoning for what superficially, appears to be no more than a sad death. This is the ideal, however, watch carefully. The enemy has been known to willingly allow us extra provision to attack our patients during difficult times, with the result inexplicably leading to a shocking reversal of heart, and a heightened and enduring connection to their "saviour". Such acts have truly been known to occur and you must avoid this at all costs. However, if this occurs, you may simply suggest to your boy after the dark time has passed that the connection with his higher power was simply a coping mechanism, and now that all is restored to normal, he can resume his usual way of thinking.

But I wish to refocus on the human experience of mourning the passing of someone they know and love. The common emotional vulnerabilities associated with such an experience are true pleasantries for us. During such times, they are irritable, short sighted and consider themselves the centre of the universe. It is so easy for them to cut themselves off from compassion, selflessness, patience and sometimes even love. Better yet, during this time, it is advantageous for you to suggest in his mind seemingly harmless activities to cope with the negative emotions, only to have incidentally created a habit which, with some persistence, addiction or compulsive behaviours may be borne.

Of course, many of these behaviours are sources from the human's fundamental and quite primal fear of a physical passing, otherwise known to them as death. You are fully aware that since the unforeseen and devastating act of sacrifice made by the enemy's son, the current reality of our universe sees human's easily able to access their place amongst their creator. This of course, as you are aware from your training, is the essence of why your duties are now so much more important. Gone are the days when we were able to simply toy with them, knowing full well that the original sin, stained across their heart, would render them ticketed for a swift departure to our home of fire and fear.

The benefits for a human to witness a loved one die is to watch their emotional constitutions erupt in sadness and disrepair. They feel as if all happiness, joy, light and innocence has been taken from the world. Many are ripped from their status quo left in a cold, dark unknown. They fear how they will navigate the world without the physical presence of their beloved. How short-sighted they are! So many are, in their moment of their manic delirium, simply unable to fathom the simple transient transformation their loved one's soul has taken. They are blinded by their emotions and this renders them particularly vulnerable.

This is when you strike. Begin the age-old suggestion in his mind of "if God loved me he wouldn't put me in this pain, therefore he is not real". What is particularly enduring about this fallacy is that it is self fuelling. The more he begins to feel and believe it, the more he will look for evidence to prove the abstraction. It is a lens that he can view the world and once firmly placed over this perspective eye, is deliciously difficult to remove. You must do all you can during this time of duress to construct this idea into his mind now.

By achieving this, it takes drastic action from the enemy to undo such damage. I am concerned that he is engaging in deep prayer to his creator for support and love during this time. Such an act may ruin any chance of a ploy as the one described above. Next time he engages in the act of ethereal communication, do all you can to distract him and ground him in the physicality of his body. As he kneels, have his knees jolt in discomfort, have him consider present woes or woeful recollections. I do not care what avenue he takes. The objective is to make him think he has given his pain and grief over to the enemy, when in fact all he has done is complete a moment of wasted, mildly uncomfortable and fruitless thought.

During this time, do not allow him at any point to give his naturally occurring pain to the enemy. This singular act corresponds to and touches on one of their strongest weapons against us. That is their ability to offer supreme protection to any soul who offers itself to the will and design of their creator's plan. By committing such an act, they instantly become impervious to any attacks, because they KNOW what you are doing. He will begin to notice your tricks and ploys, detect and recognise the patterns of your temptations and suggestions. In this moment of pain, the enemy's knowledge of what you do will be made known to the soul, and you are finished. Do not allow this to happen Incendus.

Yours with affection,

Maniacus

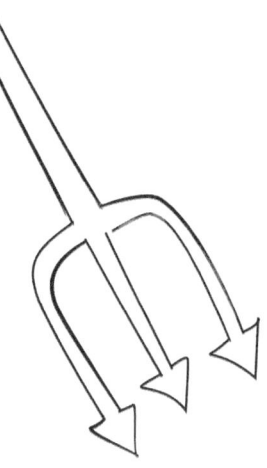

DOMESTIC VIOLENCE

My Dearest Incendus,

I understand the conflict you have mentioned to me in your previous letter. I must say, your ambition and plan to convert your man from a husband to a wife striker is honourable, but I doubt your chances. I say this because he is not prone to rage, as some are. I will tell you a story of one past soul I was successful in acquiring.

My boy was kind and normally peaceful in heart. It was incredibly difficult to navigate to any form of sinful activity. There was no part of him that derived a thirst for aggressive activity. He was, however, overly protective of his objects and loved ones. And this was enough. When he met his woman, I carefully and intricately worked to establish his perception of her as not a being, equal in honour and glory to him, but as his most prized possession. Precious yes, but not an autonomous and independent being. Every time she suggested an idea or perspective different or counter to his, instead of allowing him to process the unexpected dialogue as a normal and healthy part of a relationship, I had him categorise it as a threat to his masculinity and control of his life.

At first, you will gently begin to suggest that a push or unkind shove during disputes will not cause any harm. He will reject these at first, but each time the thought is placed it gains reasonability and justification as he becomes accustomed to it. Eventually there will be a fight so annoying and so frustrating to him that he will finally commit the act. Remember, he will inject heavy amounts of justification and excuses for why he did what he has done and that it was not his fault.

At this point, allow your human to construct an alternate reality, operating within his own mind, where he is self-serving and able to justify any reason to bring harm to his significant other. We are fully aware what the laws of his physical land instruct regarding such an act, and this will allow you to convince him to keep it to himself and not seek help of any kind from it.

Remember Incendus, the act of violence from one human to another is ancient, nearly as old as sin itself. When Cain struck Able, it was in fact, the first act of domestic violence.

It is an act that, before original sin, did not exist in any universe. Technically speaking, the act is in defiance of what it is to be human, and by having them engage in the behaviour, it takes them further away from who they are, and by extension, from their Creator. Do you see it now? You are harming the enemy when they harm each other. This is the weakness of the other side, and you would do well to have him drift down this unhallowed path.

By extension of this sin, many other suddenly seamingly extreme acts are available to the patient. By convincing him to cause harm in one particular way it inexorably allows for a justification of other harms to occur since we've already adjusted and contorted the perspectives of the individual to commit one form. Humans love to adapt what they know into activities that are unknown to them.

One example is in relation to animals. Take the scenarios of the barking dog, the chirping bird or the lazy cat. Any of these creatures may in some way, shape or form become annoying or frustrating to your individual at one point. If you catch them in a moment of vulnerability, you can strike with a deep impulsive desire to bring harm to another as a reckoning of control and a desire to be master of one's own fate. Of course, this naturally goes against their very essence and is to be encouraged. However, once again, ensure that you are strategic about when you have him indulge in such a primal edge.

I hope I have made the essence of my correspondence to you now abundantly clear. It is that many sins are cousins of one another, and it is your duty to allow them to be disguised as simply one to ensure he does not feel like he is committing various atrocities. He should be made to think he is simply experiencing one form of relief or weak point or cheat day or whatever he needs to tell himself to make the acts seem small. It is your responsibility to ensure he accepts this in any way that you deem necessary to make him or move him from having any inclination to resolving it.

As to your other inquiry regarding his capacity to derive violence from others, it is well known that any sin enacted by someone that is precursored by another individual, appears on their final tally, and therefore is of course to be encouraged. Hatred breeds hatred as we know, and it is your responsibility to position him so the seeds of any moments of distrust, anger or otherwise any form of discord amongst his family, friends and community set him down the dark and hurtful road. This race of filth is so easily susceptible to our suggestions, that it is simply immoral for us to not engage and to abuse this right to behold.

Yours with affection,

Maniacus

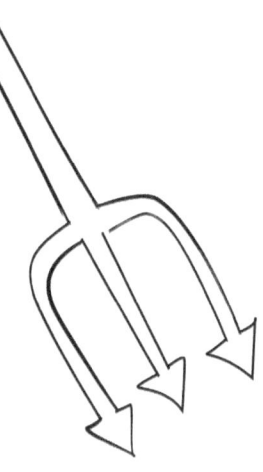

MONEY AND RELATIONSHIPS

My Dearest Incendus,

You have been correct to bring this important development regarding your growing boy to my attention. Let us assess.

He is currently continuing his studying while engaging in many hours of work, has begun to involve himself in multiple co-curricular activities and is getting married soon. All the while he is desperately fleeing your once well held positions of addictive tenancies. He is under immense pressure and thus, is currently at a crossroads.

I pray to our father that you are making use of this vulnerable time in his life to flare up any reason to create discourse in his heart that otherwise you would not have the opportunity to do. You mention how he is struggling to consolidate his feelings towards money and general finances with his wife-to-be. Ah. Money. Our old and reliable friend and ally.

It is well established that our persistent suggestion to humans to pursue the material riches of this world is a fundamental technique to capture souls. It is the allure of physical comfort, the carnal desires of aesthetic beauty and the selfish ambition of the corrupt beings which all contribute to the ease of us so easily and continuously compelling humans into the illusion of happiness from wealth and objects. They can be totally hypnotised and transfixed upon the desire and possibility of more in the future, that often we have found they never look up in the present to appreciate what they do have.

This blindness is effectively imputed on the patient with a simple avoidance of gratitude. The next time he receives something of value, say a birthday present, have him wonder its cost, value, use, functionality, any potential insidious indirect reason to have received, what he may have to do in return, and any other irrelevant considerations, any other thought other than one of gratitude and love. By maintaining persistent pressure on this way of thinking, you will eventually form within him a habit to consider everything in this life in this way. It is a trick as old as the humans themselves. Take Babylon and their pathetic attempt to conquer God. It was a golden age for us. Ah to relive the ease in which we could toy with them.

Next, begin the subtle and subdued attempt to detach and become unfamiliar with the usual and correct thought and emotional responses that should usually be experienced when blessings are delivered by the enemy. For example, next time someone completes a random act of kindness, have him entertain the act as some kind of insidious ploy by the person to have him "owe" something in return for a later date. Alternatively, you may have him believe that the individual committing the act only did so for a self seeking reason, or to make himself feel ok about helping someone else. The concept is to sway him from considering the selflessness of the moment and resisting the urge to pass it on to others.

Once complete, you will have eventually gained access to new and exciting resentments which would have previously been unattainable to you. This includes the aforementioned issues in consolidating his thoughts around money and how his less financially secure fiance is entering his life and therefore gaining access to the money that he has according to his own concepts, work hard turn. The sinister and selfish thought is brilliant because it also accompanies the occasional feelings of guilt and shame which, as we know, separate the patient from the enemy as well as companion and makes the issue appear larger in his head, increasing the effect of this strategy.

All of this points to the general direction of allowing all the painful and self seeking aspects of his mind to guide his decisions and actions. This is made easy by utilising the pathway of riches, and in particular, money, because the pursuit of it is both promoted and prioritised heavily in the society where he lives, and is easily disguised as a venture rooted in security and goodwill, when you of course know in many cases, it is anything other than this. Also, when they place value and status on how much money they have, it is logical that the next and simple experience to catalyse is envy and jealousy for those who have more, elitism and belittlement for those who have less, and competitiveness for those who have the same. Satisfaction is simply not a possible outcome.

Which brings me to the point about his wife-to-be. As I'm sure we will discuss in the future, male humans maintain the corruptible flaw of objectifying and dismissing their female counterparts. Their inherent and primal sense of pride actively seek different means of raising themselves up above all those around them, including even those they care for. This can be the case with money. Men's obsession with size translates nicely, and the amount of money being larger than his new lady will easily render him susceptible to all the abovementioned vices.

So, what are my specific and recommended next steps?

Simple, during the marriage preparation, where many expenses and fees are due, have his inevitable and reluctant release of money be somehow a nefarious act against him, delivered by his wife. Have him actually resentful and wickedly offended by the very act of his physical wealth over hers. Humans are truly capable of descending to such depths.

Yours with affection,

Maniacus

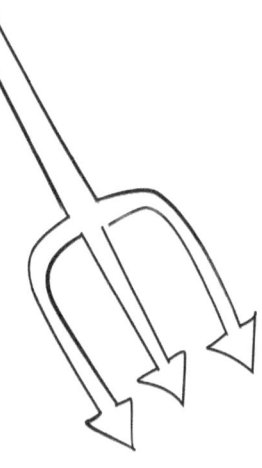

MARRIAGE AND THE DANGERS OF THE SACRAMENT

My Dearest Incendus,

Do not give me your excuses for your failure to stop your soul's matrimony to an individual who will obviously be detrimental to our cause. She brings a balance and solution to so many of his natural, and artificially embedded vices, and you will find that many usual routes to suggestion and perverted inceptions now fail due to the new and powerful motivations, confidences and consequences that are all incorporated into the title of spouse. I will touch on this in a moment.

This is all the more frustrating because you were doing so well. I note your clever and well timed bait and switch technique successfully resulting in your patient relapsing with his substance as well as other compulsive behaviours. I am glad to see the academy is still obviously instilling within its pupils traditional, ancient but effective techniques such as this. And all of this three weeks before his wedding and while his fiance was away. I'm sure you were prematurely revelling in his pain, experienced through guilt, shame, fear and hopelessness as well as the equally, if not more devastating emotional impacts his actions had on his family and his wife-to-be.

There are so many things you and your colleagues should have done at this point that you did not do. The automatic resentments and hardened hearts that you curated within those nearest to him should have been doubled down and reinforced, hidden from the healing light of their creator, and festered in the sanctimonious elitism that is so easily formed in the hearts of christians. Instead, they have shown signs of the damned healing abilities of the enemy to undo the emotional harms caused, and they are talking to him once again and even showing signs of expressing love.

You also did not push your patient further into the furnace of despair for his actions, and instead allowed him to persistently maintain a hope in what he calls God, to keep him and hold him safe during this pivotal time in his life, which is of course what he has done. Do not think that this qualifies you for a pardon or exemption from your due punishments. You know full well our kind to not engage in such abominable practice. This is why your words and attempts at mitigation are futile.

Let me explain to you why you juniors are punished every time a sacrament is completed by their patient. When a human participates in a physical practice, ceremony or ritual which includes the imparting of divine grace from their creator, or what they call the "holy spirit" to them, it is called a sacrament. It is a direct line to the enemy, and the damage that this creates can have repercussions for years to come. I should not have to be telling you this. In fact, I am now disturbed that you even momentarily forgot our ways and dared ask for any form of absolution. I will be writing to your head demon and request that your punishment be doubled. How else will you learn Incendus?

Let me discuss the specific repercussions of you allowing him to complete the sacrament of matrimony.

In a phrase, the act sanctifies and blesses the unification and inauguration of a new church. This church, or new family, are clearly instructed, sworn and blessed to live as the enemy did while he was on Earth. This is, of course, the total and utter antithesis of what our desired outcome for the patient is. The three aims of the marriage are:

1. Cooperation between the betrothed;

2. Procreation;

3. Protection against adultery and fornication.

Unfortunately for you, as much as they were already potentially protected from all your attacks, they have most certainly been blessed by the spirit of the enemy to proceed into a partnership that primarily is mandated to bring goodness into the world. I remind you, you allowed this to happen.

Now, as I briefly mentioned before, this partner of his has proven this past decade to present as a major and enduring threat to our capacities and potential to capture this soul. She brings a calmness, peace and consideration to the many moving parts of your boy's life that he would otherwise be completely inept at generating for himself. There are the obvious logistical difficulties now that he is a married man. He is finally able to engage in the sanctified practice of love making. No longer can you launch attacks suggesting that waiting for married life is just too laborious and he should lay with his fiance and thus, go against the nature of their designated period of chastity. This is a dangerous time. He will now move into a home with what I fear is a negative influence. She will continue to bring him an abundance of happiness and joy, and this results in less opportunities of attacks when he is compromised, similar to what occurred with his relapse. I offer no words of advice for now. I do not wish to present you with hope for your case at this time. You must sit and wallow in your failure. Feel the pain of the lashes and extractions and in that time, renew your efforts to complete your father-provided opportunity for glory and pride. To bring this boy home.

Prepare yourself young one. I have heard the torture techniques have been amended and strengthened to reflect the recent deficit in the yield of souls.

Yours with affection,

Maniacus

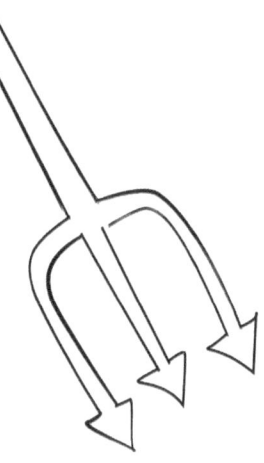

LOSING TRUST FOR GOD AND HIS PLAN FOR US

My Dearest Incendus,

I understand that as your patient settles into his new life, and the glow and shine of his nuptials dim and fade, there is the potential for you to pose right and relevant questions. Have him quietly inquire to himself:

- Have I made the correct decision?

- Why is she so (insert any arbitrary fault of the wife)?

- Could I have done something better with my life?

Needless to say, as I have mentioned to you many times before, ensure he does not build enough confidence to share these abstractions with another person. We have established that the act of a human sharing their deepest thoughts and ideas with another person diminishes or increases their value, depending on their true cause for concern in reality. In this case, by having him perpetually cycle through these questions, they will build in size and effect, much like the kindling of a fire. Small and harmless at first, but capable of true destruction if left unattended.

Your ability to incept such concepts is determined by the human being's capacity to commit an act so fundamentally stupid, that it permits us to access his own ability to form opinions and make decisions. What is this ability I hear you inquire? It is their capacity to forget to trust in their creator and believe that they are in control of what is and what will happen to them. The nature of this fallacy has proven so useful, that we have seen even the purest of souls be suddenly pulled down into our house because of this flaw.

Of course, the most immediate advantage of a human beginning to lose faith in their divine plan is the ease in which they can dismiss, judge, or even resent their creator, because of something that happens or has happened to them or someone else. Take for example your patient's grandmother experiencing a physical death not days before his wedding. At this highly emotional juncture, you should have pushed with all you have to pronounce that his "God" simply would not do something as cruel or horrid or untimely or any other type of nonsense, and therefore he either does not love his creation or simply does not even exist. This moment is absolutely critical. As he settles into this sometimes confronting thought, go gently, and slowly suggest that perhaps it is best he consider troubling situations without the inclusion of his higher power's involvement.

His decision to engage in this independent practice may be fueled by rage, sadness, an egotistical presumptuous viewpoint of how he believes the world order should stand, and most of all, selfishness; that nothing of pain should ever come to him, his family or friends. His extremely limited and shortsighted viewpoint regarding the reason the enemy commits acts of pain and suffering in the world is a most useful condition of our warfare that you must never forget. Humans do not see the spiritual landscape that we non-physical beings reside. They have no absolute physical evidence that we exist, and this is an advantage that we must never overlook.

Returning to your patient's current situation, the conditions suggest a much subtler approach to detaching him from his ethereal master. This is where you must abide by the practices of Luke-warmness. A fascinating phenomenon which many humans are susceptible to. Allow me to explain.

Consider a frog which is due to be boiled and eaten. If the water is already boiling and the frog is placed into it, it will of course immediately jump out. However, if you place the frog into luke-warm water, it will find comfort and remain happy as you continue to slowly heat its surroundings. By the time the frog realises it is in danger, it is too late, for the flesh of its limbs are already disabled and it cannot escape its impending death.

In your case, this translates in having the boy decide he does not need to ascribe to the teachings of this creator on small, seemingly negligible items. Perhaps he does not need to assist his wife with the cleaning anymore. Maybe he can have a conversation with another individual which may be considered flirtatious. Is his wife saying or doing something that he decides he does not have the patience to endure anymore? These are but a few scenarios that may be accessed when he is in this state of luke-warmness, where his trust for the enemy above is diminished and his idleness of the home environment is monotonous and "safe".

It is important that he does not remember his matrimonial vows or else you will be undone in this attack. I hope you are astute enough to now understand the forgetful nature of these stupid creatures, whose souls we so ruthlessly hunt and crave. They are capable of living through experiences that for us eternal creatures, would render a lesson perpetually learned. But not them. They are able to make the same mistakes time and time again. Have him forget, Incendus. Have him forget where he has come from and the life he has led in the past, the simple beauties and abundant blessings he has in the present and the great and infuriatingly hopeful future his life currently has.

Yours with affection,

Maniacus

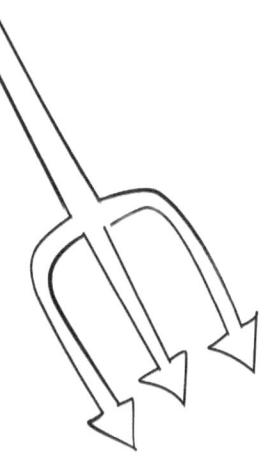

POOR HEALTH

My Dearest Incendus,

I am glad to hear of his poor health at present. Of course, do take this development with a grain of salt. The enemy, still in full control of all aspects of your patient's fate, has most likely done this for a reason. It is your responsibility to establish what that reason is, and prepare a suite of counter attacks to either block or mitigate the potential effects of what they have planned for him. What type of illness is it? I require a full medical report outlining all diagnoses and prognoses, and will arrange to deploy auxiliary assistance to ensure maximum distress and adequate messaging of hopeless pain for the human. I will expect you to repay my most helpful actions in due course. One human lifetime's personal servitude shall suffice.

My reaction to your news is only so because we have seen time and time again a transformation of the spiritual disposition of a person as they experience persistent and ongoing ailments. These reactions to such personal struggles are as multivariate and unique as there have been humans on the Earth. One thing we do know is that the extent and duration of the sickness does not correlate with the likelihood that they will collapse under the pain of the experience and succumb to our messages of hopelessness and pain. On the contrary, our best minds are still attempting to explain how some of the enemy's most distinguished accomplishments were borne out of the greatest levels of pain and suffering.

Alas, the opportunities to exacerbate their physical pain and from this, mount an attack on his mental health, is simply too inviting to miss. We are an opportunistic species. It is our nature to seek out the many weaknesses of humans and nurture them until they are fully blown defects of character or vices.

In an ideal scenario, you will want to do three things:

1.   Have him doubt the benefits of the sickness

It is important to note that we cannot empathise with the humans when considering how sickness affects a sentient being. Mortality renders the act of being unwell substantially more significant for humans because it represents the continued failure of the life-giving vessel which is their body. This is compounded when they are terminal, but for now it does not appear to be the case with your patient. As mentioned, there is a confounding and contradictory set of potentially disastrous effects for our side if you allow the enemy to enter his mind and have him look upward for peace and gratitude as opposed to around in pessimism and doubt. By not nurturing the seeds of uncertainty and distrust that you will of course lay as a result of the vulnerability he has because of the pain he is in, you run the risk of allowing the enemy to manifest themselves as the sole source of comfort and relief in his heart, forcing him to flee to their embracing arms. This also sometimes has future repercussions beyond the sickness, which is why it is critical you do not allow it to happen. Please refer to my previous correspondence regarding losing trust in God.

2.   Use this opportunity to have him become self-seeking and self-pitying

This is an easy win for our side because all you are required to do is facilitate and protect a corrupt but naturally occurring human tendency. Almost all humans cannot help but become more self-indulgent when they are unwell. They lose track of the world around them and their own physical sensations of well-being, or the lack of it, is heightened. Now this is not to say that the enemy does not allow or sometimes even endorse human's ensuring they sometimes take time to care for their own bodies and minds. It is obsessive, indulgent and in many cases, ironically destructive behaviour that we are seeking. Their detachment from reality exacerbates their own situation, as they hinder themselves from seeing how so many others on the planet are more greatly suffering. Which brings me to my final recommendation.

3.   Let him forget all that he has to be grateful for

As I have explained several times over the years, humans are, despite what they are capable of, naturally disposed to selfish and ungrateful thoughts. They are inclined to seek out what is wrong or imperfect and to complain, gossip or resent the thing. Difficult and unnatural it is for them to consider and reflect on those details of their life which are perfect, gifted, fortunate, enduring, deserved, bestowed or granted. It is infinitely more challenging when they are unwell and in pain. According to their subconscious, the practice of gratitude does not serve any purpose, and instead, superfluously consumes bandwidth. On the contrary, we have seen individuals experience devastating transformations of mindset and connection to people, place and creator all through the simple habit of a daily gratitude list. It is essential that you keep him focused on the pain, suffering on all personal, logistical and theoretical negatives of his life. Of course, it is a given that you should be making these suggestions throughout his life, but you will simply find it easier to source items for him to brood over. Is his wife not being as of much assistance as he thinks she should be? Has he apparently missed a potential work opportunity?

Whatever you can think of, have him focus on these instead of the fact he still has the breath of life in him.

Yours with affection,

Maniacus

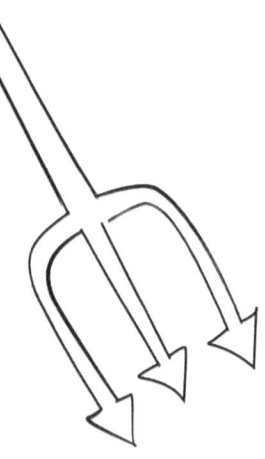

FEAR OF THE UNKNOWN

My Dearest Incendus,

Indeed you are wise to predict a potential opportunity for you to gain ground on his soul. Fear is a powerful tool to use in times of trouble. I understand he is due to have an operation soon. This of course brings with it potential opportunities for concern regarding his physical well-being, especially considering that this surgery does not improve his health but rather his vision. He would of course be second-guessing and wondering if he's made the right decision, all the while forgetting to trust it is his higher power who dictates that all happens for a particular reason.

Of course, during this time, he will be experiencing heightened dread and anxiety for what is to come, but remember along with this will undoubtedly be gratitude as well as an attempt to cling to something of solace and certainty. As I've told you before, it is paramount he does not decide to derive comfort from his creator. It will act as a notable deterrent for you when attempting any ploys which aim to sow seeds of doubt or confusion about the components of his life.

This is why I offer an important alternative to what is a growing void in your patient's heart that must be filled. It is the focus on science, technology and people that will serve as a sufficient distraction from the enduring peace that may be experienced if the boy sought out his father. Let me use a specific example.

He will soon no doubt have a particular fear that the instruments used for this procedure will fail. Specifically, that the lasers used to ablate and burn off the most superficial layers of his eyes will malfunction and cause a sudden, painful and permanent loss to his vision. So, as the thought enters his mind, you must immediately remove any defying conceptions that may calm him from it. Allow it to rise and the irrationality of it grow until he is simply bursting for a calming resolution. Then, insidiously, convince him that since these lasers are a creation of science and nothing else, it is science and the people who are operating them who will not make the mistake of causing him to lose his sight.

He should not for one moment consider that his creator will do whatever it is he has planned for him, and that within that abstraction, anything other than perpetual calm and peace towards the unknown is completely redundant.

This is what is so fascinating about the Earth stranded creatures. Their understanding of time is so intermittent and arbitrary, that they are truly capable of engaging and becoming one with their creator in one moment and at the very next completely forget and reside in the festering emotions that you are able to instill within their minds and hearts. Never forget that and never become disheartened because it is interchangeable at any one moment. It only takes a moment of weakness, a moment of forgetfulness or a moment of selfishness.

I have told you once before but I feel I must remind you of the absolutely critical point that humans cannot see what you see and they do not know what you know. Their decision to entrust the future of their lives in the perpetual care of the Creator obliges them to place faith in something they cannot see touch or engage with in any other way other than prayer and a close examination of the wonders and miracles that the enemy frustratingly showers them with at all moments of their lives. You must sympathise if you can (I know it is difficult) to consider the plain and blissful unaware nature that these humans demonstrate, sometimes completely ignorant of the might and strength that the enemy is so easily able to demonstrate during times of difficulty and strife.

Back to the example regarding his ocular surgery. If you are successful in blocking his mindframe from considering the power and potential for the creator to protect him from any harm, it is possible for you to then infuse his mind with the uncomfortable and distressing potential possibilities and outcomes of the surgery, further fuelling his fears and spiralling him into emotions of great pain, something we always strive for. This will be the case because he is simply unable to consolidate the perpetual issue that he is resting his trust within infallible and corruptible means, in other words the doctors and instruments relating to his surgery.

It is finally when they are in this vulnerable predicament that you and your colleagues are able to infest his mind free of any consequence from the enemy. They have made the decision to avoid any of the available forms of comfort and calm that he can offer. When this is done, watch them squander any remaining fleeting moments of hope, peace and joy. Worries and concerns beyond his surgery will begin to emerge and you will grow in power over his thoughts, opinions and present woes. At this point, there will be very little remaining resistance and his heart, mind and of course soul will be yours in due course. They usually end their own lives at this point because the concept of having to rely solely on logic and reason to explain all the seemingly illogical and unreasonable anomalies of the universe will induce the highly sought after existential crisis, which in some cases, has led them directly into our arms. It is certainly worth a shot.

Yours with affection,

Maniacus

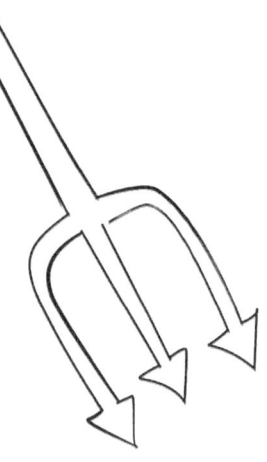

BETRAYAL

My Dearest Incendus,

The feelings of betrayal are amongst the sweetest of flavours. Bitter and potent, sour and fragrant. This experience provides a unique opportunity for you to birth, develop and exploit numerous more painful and useful traumas.

Betrayal is worse than gossip. A gossip may not necessarily harbour ill-will towards his or her victim; but a betrayer knowingly divulges information in a breach of confidence. They commit 'relational treason' by violating the trust someone has placed in them.

People are naturally inclined to trust others in good will and love. It is an interesting concept and ironic all the same that people who are trusting are also completely capable of participating in activities that break the trust of others. This is yet another fallible, incorruptible characteristic about disgusting soul bearers. It is of course vital that trust be transacted at some point in order for the act of betrayal to occur. Trust as a virtue can be abused by us through ignorance and voluntary naivety where an individual renders themselves completely vulnerable to the attacks of his or her fellow humans. This is why gullibility is an interesting and perhaps underutilised resource for you to consider.

The corruption comes when an individual decides that their needs are above the sanctity of trust of the other. The feelings prime your boy for optimal corruption and retribution. Now, when preparing the patient for betrayal, it is often advantageous to have him be expectant of unreasonable circumstances from all the people in his life. This way, we will more often experience feelings of disappointment, anger, and betrayal is often not far behind. This presumptive persona forms part of a broader lifestyle, curated by certain expectations about how things will eventuate in an individual's life.

Let us use an example from your patient's circumstances.

He has no doubt formed personal relationships with his colleagues at work. This is a frustrating inevitability which humans usually engage with. In this case, it can be used as a weak point. A vulnerability. His ambition will no doubt have him sooner or later, actively seeking and requesting some type of promotion, whether it be by title, money or power. In this instance, have him insist on one and with it, permission for him to believe that he deserves one.

Now from what you have told me of the patient, I would class him as a level 47 trust seeking individual. This suggests he has developed over the years a sense of friendship and camaraderie with his superiors. It is most likely that this feeling of true familial emotion is not reciprocated by these people and it is imperative that you do not allow him to come to realise this. Allow him to travel forth and politely but confidently place the request for increased money and watch his fall from grace as he is devastated by the negative response by his superiors.

At this critical point, fuel the momentum of his decline, reinforcing every negative emotion, thought and idea. If he is sad, permise him to manifest sadness in other aspects of his life. If he thinks that he is a failure and that, contrary to his belief, he is in fact untalented and unskilled, suggest he seek other examples of his life on how he is just that. Finally, and perhaps most importantly, when fueled by this wonderfully pained frame of mind, have him produce unhelpful and often detrimental ideas that detract from his overall life and his relationship with the enemy.

He will begin to wonder how his Creator would dare lead him down a path of such apparent injustice and treachery. This questioning and mistrust towards the enemy is exactly what we are seeking and it is found in a concentrated refined state when he is in this mindset. This is one of the reasons why keeping him like this for as long as possible is the ideal.

He will also feel sorry for himself and allow self-seeking and self-centered thoughts that otherwise would not appear in his everyday life. This will inevitably lead him to contribute less to the world and remove any chance that he engages in acts of kindness or selflessness. It truly is an advantageous time for you and it is not to be squandered.

Frustratingly, there are factions within the Enemies ranks on earth who understand that no person is equipped to be fully trustworthy and also that love in the face of the trial of betrayal is the very antidote to the negative consequences of it. In fact we have seen it written in their holy book that they are to "turn the other cheek", a disgusting act of humility despite wrong doing done on an individual.

This is a true threat to your hold on your patient, especially as he is so learned in the enemy's book. It is indeed true that we have seen years of diligent work undone all due to the resonance and acceptance of the words and wisdom provided to him by The Enemies ranks on Earth. Keep him away from these humans for as long as you can. Instead have him take the company of earthly and overly ambitious people within his professional community as opposed to his family and nourishing friends.

Most importantly, we have seen time and time again the potential for the human to exhibit enemy-like tendencies and forgive their transgressors, irrespective of whether or not they deserve it. This natural break of justice and retribution is abominable I know, yet it mysteriously has proven to undo our actions. You are warned.

Yours with affection,

Maniacus

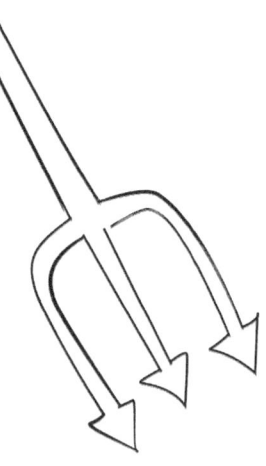

DANGERS OF PRAYER

My Dearest Incendus,

How, and what are you doing? I haven't received correspondence from you for some time and I'm not sure whether to be concerned or relieved that you are now sufficiently and appropriately engaging with your patient in a way that does not require my assistance. In any case, I wish to pass on my reflections regarding a most important issue that you must not allow to leave your grasp for a single moment. I wish to discuss the concept of prayer and the dangers it pertains to your exclusive capture of your patient's soul.

Ever since the beginning, and more specifically, since the great fall, the enemy has maintained the frustrating advantage of easy and enduring methods of communication with the humans; something that has always eluded us.

The form of communication that this has traditionally taken is extremely varied, although to this day, the most common form is that of prayer from the human to their creator. The first and most important note to make is that you have the perpetual task of strongly compelling your subject during the most ominous times of his life, that it is only a one way form of communication, simply because the enemy does not reply in way of verbal response. I know Incendus, they are stupid enough to believe that there is no one there. Once again, remember, they do not see what we see or know what we know. Their scope of their world is so limited, it is easy to confuse them, simply by exaggerating the absence of what they cannot sense with their physical bodies.

However, if you are noting that he is at a time of his life where he is trying to engage with something invisible to him, you are able to deploy several tactics that will keep him from conversing with his creator. Firstly, the next time he begins to pray, have him convinced that he's only doing so because he is in an extreme part of his life whether it be total happiness or complete devastation. This will detach himself from the concept that prayer should be conducted at all times and in every situation. Next, have him truly focus on being selfish and self-seeking in his prayers. Have him ask for things that will only benefit him as well as those he loves and knows. Do not for one moment allow him to engage in prayer for his enemies or those he does not know.

Many people have used prayer in the past as a mirror, simply going through the motions without actually trying to connect with the entity on the other end. This is similar to a journal or a letter that people write to themselves. It is not sincere and it is not meaningful. They simply do not have the capacity to comprehend who it is they are speaking to. If only they understood they had the unfathomable capacity to communicate with the creator of all things including us. Also, nearly all humans do not spend enough time in prayer. Most would not give more than a minute or two which is most fortunate for us because as we have seen, the trickiest of people to hunt are in constant communication with the Enemy.

It is important to note that due to the traditional and regimented style of Christianity that he's practicing, he will most likely recite prayers that are set for him, written by men thousands of years ago. This form of prayer is a double-edged sword and it is important that you listen to me very carefully. The contents of them are extraordinarily powerful as they express dangerous sentiments towards the Enemy that the individual would not be able to make on his own. However due to the nature that they are not his own words and that he reads them as opposed to thinks of them, it allows him to simply speak the words and not mean the words. He's able to blindly recite and officially stroke the words.

This is what you want for him. Do not allow him to compliment these prayers with deep ones.

Finally and to the note above, do not have him engage in deep, meaningful or sincere prayer, where he brings to the enemy his deep vulnerabilities of pain and suffering. He's not to learn the secret and destructive power of healing, calm, peace and love that individuals who practice thoughtful prayer experience. If you do, you may never win him back. His mind will be too strong and too preoccupied by the enemy-given serenity.

To summate what I have just said, keep his prayers short, selfish and superficial.

They do not know what they have, Incendus. The simple and uncomplicated capacity for them to directly communicate with their creator is a potential reservoir of unending peace, grace and glory for them. They can so easily fuffle themselves with small or large problems within their own lives. It is up to you to have them forget that they are but one prayer away from handing themselves over to their frustratingly forgiving creator. Do not underestimate your human if and when he engages in any attempt to pray. It is likely that he will be facilitated by his children and his other family members because our father knows that habits are caught by others, not developed individually. As a last resort, next time he feels the impulse to pray, suggest he call one of his influential friends to complain or engage in worrying gossip where he may hopefully even receive some bad advice which takes him further away from those above and closer into our warm and hungry hands.

Yours with affection,

Maniacus

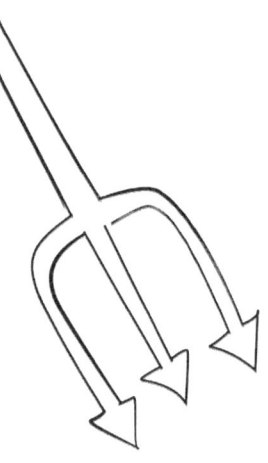

CHILDREN

My Dearest Incendus,

I am surprised to hear that your patient has become a father. I thought you had disabled his drive and hope regarding having children with the news that due to anatomical deficiencies, it would be highly unlikely they would conceive. I see you have failed to bar him from praying to his creator to allow them this 'miracle'. To have permitted this is to your shame because you've now allowed him to access a new type of love which I have already explained is our true disabling enemy-sent virtue of which there is very little we can do.

I'm sure you experienced the violent shockwave of abundant enemy-provided love, joy, excitement and celebration when his wife told him the news. No doubt you were completely disabled for most of the day from engaging in any of your usual ploys. I know this would have been the case because his desire was met with reality and whenever the enemy allows this to happen, the bond between his creator and him is usually strengthened. As he settles into the news of his pregnant wife, attempt at all costs to drive within him sentiments of anxiety, fear and confusion but most of all worry that he will lose the baby. Have him forget that his enemy has the eternal plan for him and that whatever happens it is in his best interest.

Indeed, in the lead up to the birth of his child, he will be tested by means of patience, strength of character and selflessness. We have seen many circumstances of the enemy providing an unfair abundance of all of these virtues upon the humans during this time. Your task is to buffer against these and to have him, as much as possible, sticking to his selfish ways, and suggesting thoughts self-seeking motive. Do not let him come to understand the true nature of the miracle that has been gifted him and instead, have him confused and take the entire scenario for granted.

Possibly the strongest insecurity you'll be able to engage with his fear and anxieties is his capacity to be a good father. Toy with the concept that his past is simply waiting to pounce upon his present and future and destroy any chance of him becoming a good parent. You are able to strike during the night when all he has is his thoughts and lack of sleep to fuel these anxieties. Have him question everything he knows about what it is to be a Christian, and what it is to be someone capable of bringing a person into the wild and finally someone who can do right by someone else who relies completely upon them. Let the pressure of the moment prove too much and lead them to panic and stew.

The love he will have for his child is unlike anything he has ever known, and you will not be able to touch him for a time. He'll be wrapped up in the protective cocoon of gratitude, love and adoration for both his new offspring and his creator who gifted him this blessing.

However, believe me when I say that this emotional state will not last. Is like no other. Their emotional capacity will be expanded at an unprecedented rate while simultaneously diminishing their own physical status. In other words, they will need to take care of their most precious being, whilst extremely fatigued, sore and mentally at capacity. Of course this is the perfect breeding ground for you to instigate arguments and illogical conversations with his spouse, his family and his friends. Allow him to become accusatory, fragile and insecure. I'm sure that he will do the best that he possibly can by his newborn.

You of course gain access to a plethora of many different forms of new potential resentments. For example, there may be those who wish to provide support to him. With his ego and stubbornness manipulated by you of course, you may allow him to both not accept it and also develop a hatred towards them. Similarly you may convince him that there are those people in his life who are not doing enough to support him. The premise here is to ensure that there is no singular person who is providing the exact type of presence in his life that he needs. Make it impossible for him to be satisfied by any type of love or space provided by those in his life.

His professional life will certainly take a detrimental hit and you must do your very best to translate this into a resentment towards his newborn, who you may convince is simply a burden upon his once spectacular and ever-growing career prospects. If you play all the cards correctly and in a manner that is subtle and undetectable by your patient's consciousness, you will drive him into a state of discontent and regret for engaging. This is something which is a blessing from the enemy as well as a true and incorruptible completion of something which validates his existence. He does not know how precious and rare it is to receive something that so many do not receive, Offspring. Not to mention the abundance of opportunity and potential that his child has as a result of the part of the Earth where he resides. If all goes as planned he will not be able to enjoy the true pleasures that come with fatherhood. He will also cut himself off from the opportunities to learn and grow both as a human and as a child of the Enemy.

With the accessibility of a child in the home comes an opportunity to revisit so many of life's assumptions. As the baby becomes a toddler and begins to ask questions regarding his or her place on the earth, such simple questions will require thought on behalf of your patient. On a more simple matter, have him become annoyed and infuriated by their unending questions about the world around them as opposed to being patient, calm and understanding.

Of course you had the opportunity to instil within your patient insecurities, the difficult concept of how he is raising the child, and even better insecurities about those insecurities. He will undoubtedly want to compare himself to parents who he trusts or admires. Have him invest himself with those who promote themselves and facade their strongest self on the various technological portals that he uses. Then have him compare his own capacities as a father, and translate to further resentments to himself, the child and his wife. I do trust you are witnessing a pattern of taking a normal element of human behaviour and corrupting it to serve your purposes. This is the way we operate, this is the way it has been done for thousands of years.

I hope I have made it abundantly clear to you various opportunities that stand before you as your patient enters this new phase of life. Your success will be determined by your persistent, enduring, and well-timed attacks. I do not want to hear excuses of the enemy's protection over your meat bag. He is vulnerable, more vulnerable than he has ever been in his entire life, and it will be a true indication of your capabilities as his demon to have failed to claw him back to his old habits and thoughts. As you bombard him with these ideas of old, have him too ashamed and his ego too far inflated to seek help from either the church from science or from his family and friends. Isolate him and make him feel that there is no way out.

Yours with affection,

Maniacus

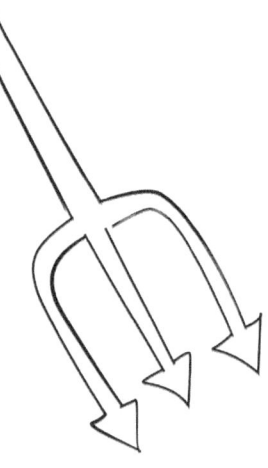

PATIENCE AND FORGIVENESS

My Dearest Incendus,

There will be times in the near future in which the patient will experience something that requires unusual levels of patience and selflessness. It is often the case that the creator for some reason, actually permits us unusual access to the boy's mind. It is almost as if he consciously desires his corrupt manifestations to be tested at various intervals. We do not know why he does this, but we do not ask questions, nor do we miss any opportunities to strike. As I was saying, during these circumstances, it is important that you blind him through mental noise and exacerbation of ego such that he does not allow himself to succumb to the temptation of a virtuous response.

To be clear, there will be occasions where his capacity to overlook, forgive, suppress or even tolerate are diminished for one of a few reasons. The scenario may be reacting with a particular insecurity or hurt of some kind. His ego may be inflamed or susceptible to particular types of people. Or he may simply be experiencing a particularly bad day and does not have his usual capacity to express patience where it is required. No matter the reason, we are all the better in these moments, as we are able to suggest thoughts and behaviours which are usually not available to us.

Let us consider a scenario where he is waiting for a friend who is late. He is standing outside in the dark and the cold and he does not know how long he will have to wait for. A wonderful opportunity to attack. There are many suggestions to make, but the skill is administering them in an order that will allow them to be built on each other, rendering him resentful and bitter. First, have him question the validity of the excuse or reason his friend has given for his lateness. Compare it against the small but rapidly growing feelings of inconvenience and allow them to bloat to the point where in fact, the excuse of the friend simply does not amount.

Next, have him run flawed subjective and highly biased exercises in his mind considering if he would do the same to his friend if he had been in his position. Of course the self righteousness of humans will elicit a superior outcome, suggesting that he would never do such a wrong under the circumstances. Importantly have him suffer under these difficult physical conditions and allow the resentment and the associated emotions take over him in such a way that even if his friend was to descend moments from this point the entire evening will be ruined and the damage would be done. This is the point that you must reach as you are gaining an enduring opportunity to remain in his heart, feeding him cold and dark cruel thoughts and sentiments into his emotions and thoughts.

At this point the patient will be in an optimal mental predisposition to lash out to his friends and family simply because he has allowed the resentment to ensue within his mind and heart. You must navigate and project his feelings into all aspects of his life to ensure maximum deflection and minimal chance of recovery. When his friend finally emerges from his home I want you to seal his lips. Fester the emotions and have him engage in notions of passive-aggression for the duration of the evening. Have him believing that he is in the right for reacting in this way.

By this point we have him in knots. His usual optimistic disposition should be yours for the taking and all that will be hidden behind a negative and sour viewpoint of the world around him. When he is in this predicament, it will be difficult for him to experience gratitude for any component of his life. He will focus only on inconveniences and minute strifes of his life such that even opportunities for him to come out of this mindset is disabled. You will have him locked in at your command. He will eventually begin to lose friends, make enemies at work, have disrupted relations with his wife and family and most importantly, hinder his capacity to maintain a strong and solid foundation With The Enemy.

The reason it is so important to ensure that his capacity to have patience is diminished is because forgiveness requires it at all steps. You're well aware that the concept of forgiveness is one which we do not recognise. However, if we did we would still not agree with its fundamental principles. It is simply not in our nature and we do not comprehend the abstraction of absolving those who have done us wrong. This is why it is absolutely critical that the patient does not experience patience because the very next step is his capacity to forgive those who do wrong by him. Take for example this very friend who has done wrong by him and has mistreated him. Your human has every right to reject any form of apology from him. You are to have him rooted in the concept that because objectively he is within his right to not forgive the individual, when he apologises, he simply should not. Do not complicate things further in his mind and allow him to derive enjoyment from the resentment that is rooted in truth to overtake him and act as a contributing factor for all of his emotional decisions. Do not allow the grace of the Enemy to enter his mind and heart and alter his perspective of the situation whereby forgiveness is granted to him on the basis that he himself is not perfect as well. Do not let him have the thoughts that although a mistake has been made here, as a human has the capacity to move beyond the fault in the same way that his creator moved on and paid the debt of the original fault.

Yours with affection,

Maniacus

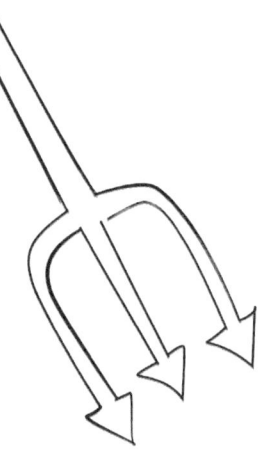

GOING TO CHURCH

My Dearest Incendus,

I am absolutely bewildered as to how we find ourselves in the predicament where your boy has re-commenced attendance at his childhood church. I thought you had effectively and physically manipulated his memories to have him consider all his history with them to be traumatic and backwards. Shame on you for committing him to enter the house of the enemy and engage in acts of treachery which move him directly away from our claws. You must now engage in damage control and you must do so quickly. Firstly, we know he is a late riser. Perpetuate this concept deeply within him such that the early starts of the Sunday Mass require an extra effort that he sometimes simply is not in a position to give.

Humans are fickle and easily taken by the present moment. Push his eyes down to his body and bring on micro pains generated from his mind, such that he has to excuse himself from committing the act of attendance to our enemy's ground. If that does not work, you must desperately seek any other excuse for him not to attend. Perhaps it is raining or he has work or other personal commitments that he must attend to and need the extra time. Perhaps his wife is unwell or his children are not cooperative and he doesn't have the potential or energy to correct their behaviour and get them ready for church. Is the house untidy and he has convinced himself that he better stay home and tidy it because he doesn't have any other time. Whatever it is do not let him get out the door.

If he finds himself entering by any other excuse, you have a host of micro manoeuvres to employ.

Redirect all of his attention to his senses. Have him consider the musty, rusty or dusty smell and the dark, dim and dingy lighting. Perhaps someone in the congregation wears perfume or has an odour that is repugnant to your patient. Tap in and have him focus on that concept, passing judgement all the while. It is to be expected that there will be members of the congregation and the church clergy who do not have the voices of our foes the Angels. Simply have him judge them for their less than perfect pitch, attracting him away from the moment of potential worship and praise. The need to stand is yet another potential distraction. Instead of allowing the weariness of his legs to strengthen his fervor towards his creator, have the thoughts of complaint, excuse and needless worry overcome him. Finally as he may not have had food to eat or water to drink, accelerate his gustatory ambitions, inducing thoughts of gluttonous satiation.

One of the many issues with your patient attending the Enemies home ground on earth is that if they received an inkling of camaraderie and community from other like-minded Christians, you are at risk of him finding solace and joy through the establishment of a new community for them. Unfortunately, this nourishment of body and soul may lead you to lose them for many years, if not completely. It is for this reason that you must have him focusing on all of the differences that he has compared to the rest of the congregation. Focus on his academic progress which differs greatly from those Elders who did not have the opportunity to learn and become qualified in the way he is. Have him concentrate on the different hobbies, interests and perspectives of small and unnecessary issues. Lastly, have him remain blind to the important and overriding connection that they share for having a belief and relationship with the Enemy.

You are well aware of the influence that other people have on your patient, particularly if they spend a large amount of time with them. There is a real threat that this will happen to your human if you're not careful. The joy and simple peace experienced by the community of a congregation can change a person, permanently. They present with the sickly sweet and wholesome disposition which may prove tempting to humans if not quelled immediately. You should work hard to steal him away to other groups of people who do not maintain such a real threat to your position in his mind and heart. Perhaps have him reacquaint with the friend who is consistently engaging in harmful practices.

For him to be engaging in the ancient traditions of his church is a physical repulsion of all of your attacks on him. He is genuinely combating all of your ploys every time he partakes in the practice. Even if he manages to derive little personal growth, spiritual development or social delight from the experience, the mere presence of his body inside the body of the enemy is a loss for you and a loss for our master and he will not tolerate it. This is because if he continues to attend out of habit, even if he does not enjoy it, he will eventually find a way to derive pleasure from something he would not have if he maintained a sporadic and habitless pattern. This is the reason you must work with the vices he already has to ensure he does not consider church as the life saving practice it truly is.

Yours with affection,

Maniacus

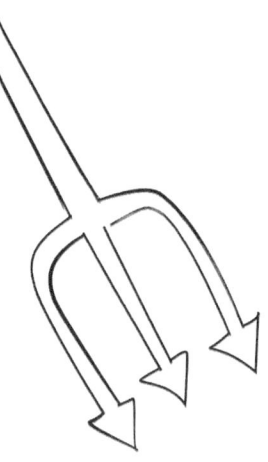

DEATH OF RELIGION

My Dearest Incendus,

Well done my offling. I am pleased to hear of the development regarding your soul's departure from his practice of religion. I also, of course, thank myself for guiding you up to this point. I trust you are aware your success is my success. It is important that you recognise what is occurring in your soul is not an anomaly. The modern era of humans you see is defined by an unprecedented crucifixion of all traditional elements relating to the worship or engagement of any kind of a god or other higher being. This is because the worship of science, which I have brought to your attention before, continues to provide temperamental answers that disguise a solid and incorruptible truth.

I note that he is simply experiencing a time of what he believes is Enlightenment above the seemingly primal practices that his religion asks of him. This is good. This organic shift in his perception for what are otherwise destructive and inexplicably detrimental thoughts to our course, is a fortunate gift of the modern era. He's obviously surrounding himself with influential people and listening to messages that are taking him away from his root of faith. Keep him along this path, but remember, you're not to push. Be slow, gentle and undetectable, for if you move too quickly, it may induce a sudden realisation in his heart and you may lose the ground you have made.

I remember the joyful time when the supernatural world brought fear and animosity towards the human race, often leading to religious wars and other forms of civil distress when the entire time, people would forget that the primary focus should have always been the simple existence of their creator. They are a foolish collection of animals who complicate and draw division between the practice of their faith and the actual belief in it.

Allow me to shift these philosophical ideas into reality. He's now listening to scientists instead of priests, he believes something exists if he can see and touch it instead of rooting his ideologies in faith. The sheer hypocrisy of this act is so easily lost on the humans. They will so easily believe in forces such as magnetism and gravity even though they cannot see, hear, touch, feel or taste it, but the concept of a realm beyond their physical realm which pertains to their soul and they're very essence of infinite existence is simply implausible and ridiculous. This is the modern era and this is where we can do our best work. What is more excellent is the population's departure from a purely spiritual life to a religious life, such that the average human can no longer differentiate between the two. The moment an individual mutters the word God, we are finding the fruits of our labour in an immediate negative reaction from many, simply because the representation of God, or in other words, the church of God, may have caused some harm to the individual, or better yet, was convinced by your brother's that they had. Irrespective of the circumstance, there is a global degradation in spiritual wisdom and enlightenment and an increase in individual entitlement and presumptuousness.

The separation of once strong and secure values which we were once unable to penetrate is a great gift that has been hard fought and hard earned by your previous Brothers. Compel them into believing that they are worshipping nothing when in fact they're worshipping either themselves, fallible science or other humans.

You must have him caught up in the current of this modern perception and even further convince him that anyone with a view that relates to faith-based reason is misinformed brainwashed and stupid. You are able to harness his level of qualification to appeal to his ego and achieve this agenda.

You can also perhaps attempt to engage in peer pressure, thanks to the extremely educated but atheist community he involves himself with. Suggest that it is detrimental to his career, both as a professional scientist and future leader of the world as it renders him biased, weak and unable to appeal to the masses as a result of his faith & religion. Do not for one moment have him think the opposite, which is the truth that with his faith and religion the enemy would supply abundant opportunities and blessing to achieve his goals. Do all you can to embed his history of his relationship with God as something that he wishes to forget, like a piece of rubbish in a vehicle thrown on a highway never to be considered again and placed as an embarrassing component of his past.

If you have played your part well, there is little chance that your patient will return to the world of his religious practices. As his life takes him away from the church, do not under any circumstances allow the various good deeds and attempts of his old friends to penetrate his heart. He is a simple creature and can easily be deterred away from the warm parts of retribution and quickly change directions back towards his creator's kingdom. I remind you as I have said for many years now, that your existence depends on the capture of the soul. Do not disappoint our father for the famine down below is on the increase and we require a fresh soul.

Yours with cautious affection,

Maniacus

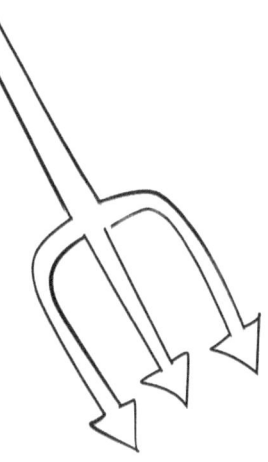

LOVE AND OTHER GOOD FEELINGS

My Dearest Incendus,

I cannot explain to you the nature of the human's experience of love. It is an abstraction that until this time, has proven incorruptible.

There are many forms of this infuriatingly obstructive phenomenon, and we do not know how it functions internally. We do know it is unfairly allocated to the sentient animals from above.

We will discuss this as the boy continues to age through his middle life.

As your training would dictate, the virtue is the single strongest weapon in the enemy's arsenal for two reasons. One, we simply do not have an antidote or reciprocal vice to balance this virtue. It is simply too overwhelmingly powerful for any of our tricks. Secondly, and most importantly, the creator himself, our sworn and horrendously benevolent enemy, is the manifestation of love in this universe. When we see the humans engaging in the practice, what we are in fact witnessing is their father from above working and operating in their lives. He gives of himself so as to bring joy and happiness into their lives. We simply cannot answer such a manoeuvre.

You are left with any opportunity to confuse other emotions for love. The most useful and powerful example is lust. As a young man, your patient is particularly inclined to experience great bouts of this emotion and through this, you are able to subtly disguise particular components of his feelings under which this vice, invades the realm of love. You will have to be inconspicuous however, as it is no easy feat to convince an individual that one emotion is another. However, you are fortunate that lust brings with it a bewitching and thought-disabling property, rendering you capable of completing this trick.

If you are in the unfortunate position of witnessing your patient engage in feelings of true and genuine love, despite it's all encompassing transformative power, here are some harm minimisation practices for you to consider. The first is harnessing the pattern that he is experiencing towards something and redirecting it from virtue to vice. Allow me to explain. He may love his wife so passionately that when someone approaches her and is suggestive of romantic intrigue in any way, his passion can be guided carefully by your manipulative fingers into jealousy. He may be so invested and blinded by love for his country he does not see the cries of those who are not his people. Finally, the protective love that he may have for his child may be so great that his anxiety and fears around danger may lead him to become aggressive or obsessed with any harm that may come to her.

I hope you can see here that it is not the emotion of love you are able to manipulate. Do not try. It is far too powerful. What you are able to attempt manipulation of are the associated auxiliary emotions which fuel his love. They are truly stupid creatures in their misunderstanding of what they have pulsing through their veins. They would go so far as to even sometimes consider love as a weakness, pulling people's interactions into acts of self sabotage and a reduction of their individual potential. It is important you have him consider these thoughts as often as you can, especially considering he is such an ambitious person.

Of course we have the other annoying but not as dangerous sentiment of contentment. You will know that your patient is experiencing this when he's accepting and open to situations that he would otherwise find annoying, frustrating or intolerable. He has a smile on his face, a chuckle in his breath and a spring in his step. It is honestly revolting to observe. However, here's what I suggest as the antidote. A distant cousin of contentment is lukewarmness which is a friend of ours in that in its subtlety, may lose motivation, a spark in their faith and appreciation for what they have just as slowly as water boils on a pot.

Other positive feelings to minimise and reduce during a patient's life is one of enthusiasm, joy and humour. Not many humans recognise that the enemy fervently encourages times of laughter and simple enjoyment of funny experiences. We do not comprehend such concepts as humour, however we do understand the potential damage it may have as you attempt to secure your boy with negative thoughts. Levity has been shown to increase your patience and resilience to such pessimism, and you must work fervently to instil within him an unnecessarily high level of seriousness and misplaced reverence. This will ensure you minimise the occasions where he is brought to simple joy and thus, closer to the enemy.

This will be a difficult task for you as your soul appears to present as a joybringer and a maker of laughter. Perhaps you can employ the technique of having him consider himself too old or too important to create content that brings simple pleasures to those around him. By doing so, he will begin to judge others who deliver something that he gives so easily and you will therefore be able to promote jealousy and envy, simply by convincing him that to bring oy, laughter and light is to be immature. I wish to know how successful you are in this venture. Our food stores are low, Incendus. I require further reporting.

Yours with affection,

Maniacus

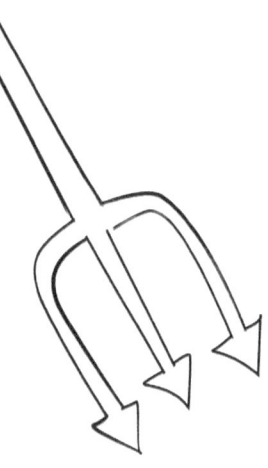

STRESS AND MENTAL HEALTH

My Dearest Incendus,

I note your boy's desire to do more with himself. By all means! Let him. What you are witnessing is an undeniable existential dilemma. He has deluded himself to think that he will successfully somehow "justify his existence" by engaging in as many activities as possible, just to increase the possibility that we will be remembered on the Earth. This is a fortunate circumstance. This mindset suggests that he will only do good deeds if he is praised for it by future generations, not simply because it is the right thing to do, or that it is what his creator has commanded of him. This dichotomy is potent enough to defile even the most extraordinary of achievements, because their motivations will be based in selfishness and pride. They will have built themselves on unstable ground and, like all men, they will crumble.

Take for example his continuous pursuit of leadership positions. Now remember, his natural inclination and passion towards such roles in his life are gifts from the enemy, designed to assist him in fulfilling his forsaken purpose on Earth. This does not mean that they can be manipulated and exploited to suit our purposes. In this case, it appears he is engaging in compulsive and inappropriate commitments to as many positions as possible, hoarding opportunities because he feels important with multiple titles, all the while not completing them appropriately because he is so time poor. This is a case of a misguided and misuse of natural abilities and it serves you well because they are easily turned away from their creator's provision of warmth and comfort upon alignment with his plan for them.

Something important to note is that each human is equipped with a certain amount of resilience to stressful situations. In this case, your patient has a high resilience. However, that does not mean he's not immune to bouts and episodes of anxiety inducing situations, catalysed by you of course. Take for example the distress he has from moving from one home to another. As he is now quite senior in his life, having responsibility for many aspects of his community, you are required to exacerbate each particular one and build them up in his mind. Of course while doing so, you will need to remove any thought that he takes his concerns to the enemy's alter. Do not suggest that you deal with each one individually but rather attempt to take them all on at once in an effort to be efficient.

Of course, there are different forms of stress that can be found in different parts of his life. The most common example is that of financial stress. As he naturally has concerns about the future well-being of his family, he may wonder if times of strife financially speaking may come upon his children. Once again, the simple fact of the matter is that the enemy does have a plan for him that we will never know. However it is your responsibility to ensure he forgets this as often as possible. Allow him the chance to dive into the potential implications and consequences of unforeseen financial burden. Another one may be through the unexpected attack on one of his family or friend's health and well-being. Your patient is annoyingly caring and will want the best for all individuals. You may manipulate this in his mind by having him over-care, and from this drive, concern about where their life is heading.

The feelings of stress and anxiety are unnatural to the human body. Stress has been known to serve as a helpful aid in bringing sickness and pain not just mentally but physically too. With this in mind, attempt to have him absorb the stress of others around him as well as regarding matters that don't even concern him. With any luck, physical predisposition and with persistent determination may allow you particular powers which the modern world are now calling mental health illnesses. By no fault of their own, a patient may present

141

you with an opportunity to be in great joy, sadness, anger, pain or sometimes no emotion at all in a way that is not usually possible without neuronal instability. I encourage you to poke around his mind and determine if he is a candidate for such an opportunity.

We are fortunate in that the church has done wonderfully horrendously in assisting the children of the enemy in coming to terms with their various mental incapacities. They have turned away and vanished so many of them before and for that reason it is important that he concentrates on this if ever he is experiencing one of the afflictions. Hopefully he will use this and keep these aspects of his life away from the clergy, his religious friends and his father. They are such Fools. They do not know that the enemy is particularly kind and loving to those who struggle with mental ailments.

The truth of the matter is that he's able to work miracles with them if they devote their pain to him, ask and surrender to his will. Do not let him come to understand that this is an important mechanism by which they can be alleviated of their afflictions. Hide from him the concept that the enemy considers him perfect in every way despite their infinite floors. As we well know, they are made in his image, despite their downfall. Focus on promoting the apparent inconceivable and inoperable levels of harm and degradation that he has, thus making it impossible for him to approach the enemy with a desire to have him healed.

Yours with affection,

Maniacus

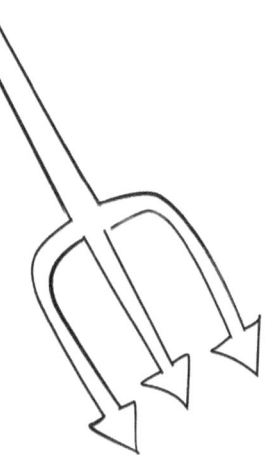

LONELINESS AND LONGING

My Dearest Incendus,

Humans engage in various activities which are completely foreign and unfamiliar to us, yet we suggest to them to feel this way because it lures them away from the enemy. These are namely, loneliness and longing. Let us look at the former first.

The standard human is most naturally comfortable when surrounded and accessible to other like minded friends. They seek to be part of a "tribe". This is why they attempt to experience friendships, relationships and other connections. Some can take it or leave it, others crave the tender touch of a lover or the loving affirmations of a friend. It appears your patient is no different. It is derived from a much older and very primal desire to "fit in" with those around them and derive their own opinions from those who they trust. With these unequivocal facts, here is what I would suggest you do with your patients longing for friends and other relationships.

In his desperation to surround himself with others, have him lower his standards and allow bad influences into his life through people who are well under our control. It is an opportunity, Incendus, for you to satisfy his loneliness with people who will provide temporary relief, but inevitably leave him lonelier and hungry for any form of affection once again.

What is even more excellent is that once they do this, you will find that they begin to emulate those who they surround themselves with. This proves to be an excellent opening for you to bring about appropriate changes in his life.

As he enters the final stages of life, he will begin to look for new opportunities he feels he has missed out on account of the good and decent life he has mostly decided to lead, much to your shame.

Perhaps it would be wise for you to instil within him resentments towards his closest, for not allowing him to experience life in the extravagant, overly exuberant way that he would have if he was living his life alone. Of course we know this is not true, but then again that is the basis of resentment. Something must be based in mistruth.

Loneliness grows within the heart of a human who does not know that they never are truly by themselves in the universe. This is one of the many factors that makes them so fickle and weak. On a planet with over 8 billion people, and the capacity for them to reach out to hundreds of people within the network, they are able to convince themselves that no one has an interest in wanting to help or simply communicate with them. This is made all the richer considering the modern technological advances which makes so many people available at the touch of a finger.

Alas, you know your patient is lonely because their internal spirit is cold and in many ways, frightened. This is when you can launch a million attacks and keep attempting to separate the knowledge that the enemy is in fact right with him, surrounding him, for as long as you can.

On the topic of longing, the difference here is that the patient usually ascribes something that they want that they currently do not have. This can be anything from a material object, something professionally superior to what they currently have or a loving touch.

It is completely within the nature of a human to experience longing for many things. Your role is to promote and enhance feelings of longing for things that will bring him closer to us. The list is endless. It is important that you focus on situations that he will never be able to experience in his current life, an example perhaps being with another person, and infecting his mind with the concept. With any luck, he will fixate on the idea and his obsession may lead to longing. This is most advantageous as it opens the capacity for him to resent what he currently has, despite it being a blessing from the enemy. This in itself provides the opportunity for him to resent his creator himself for not giving him access to what he is desiring.

Take for example his colleague who has been frustrating him at work receiving the promotion that he was so desperately longing for. You would immediately of course be able to easily and instil in his heart a strong and immediate resentment to God for giving him the capacity to have longing for something that was not given to him. Despite his training in the enemy's camp, you must do your best to manipulate his emotional demeanour and have him forget that for some reason or another, the dreadful enemy of light, benevolent and overwhelmingly loving towards these creatures, provides them with the exact emotional, social, professional, personal and most importantly spiritual experiences with the best opportunity to enter his kingdom.

Remember, make sure that they do not come to realise this, otherwise all will be lost.

Yours with affection,

Maniacus

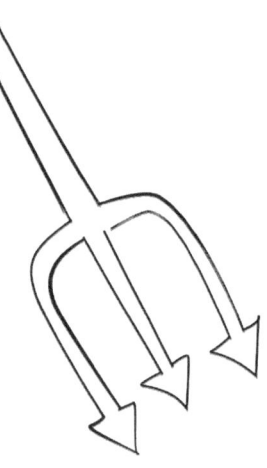

PRESUMPTIVENESS

My Dearest Incendus,

It has been many years since our last correspondence. I worry that you are not taking your position seriously, unless you are experiencing a time of productivity in which case I am satisfied with your silence . Your subject is entering his older years now and his thought systems are solidifying, which can either be an advantage or obstacle for you, depending on how much work you have done to this point . A component of his disposition that is likely changing is a sense of elitism due to his belief that he knows better than anyone younger than him as a result of the years he has lived on the Earth.

This is a hilarious development that we find in the oldest humans, simply because they convince themselves that they are most certainly as wise as they will ever be and therefore cannot learn anything new. It is imperative that you use this human floor to your advantage. The next time he is reading the bible, the next time he is receiving advice from another person, activate within him the trigger that in some way or another he already knows the information being delivered to him. In this way you will hinder his capacity to improve upon his spiritual life, but allowing you greater access to his mind and heart.

This is especially made sweeter if he identifies as a Christian. He may act as a terrible example of what the supporters of the enemy are supposed to be, thus keeping others away from joining their course. It truly is a wonderfully useful device if manipulated correctly. His mindset and his perspective on many components of his life will be hazed with a sort of pessimistic presumption and expected tone such that it is extremely difficult for him to enjoy many of life's blessings, which their creator frustratingly floods them with at any moment of any day.

From these resentments and other bedevilments, it is easy for you to insert yourself into his mind and squander the potential for gratitude and humility. Your aim here is to foster a sense of grumpiness, crankiness, unkindness, which are all close neighbours of selfishness and cruelty.

Let us use an example. Perhaps in the coming months and years he's met with a business opportunity that in reality is new and unexplored for him. As he is already a business owner and has experienced success in various ventures, activate his ego and suggest that he is too far beyond potentially engaging with this new avenue and that he in fact has nothing to gain.

It is important for us to discuss the strong potential that an individual's ego may have on serving your purposes. It is common that many humans,especially men, may have had at one point, been on the path of righteousness but turned away unexpectedly because some element of their pride, stubbornness or entitlement inhibited that path leading them to wander back towards us. You truly are in a position to convince him that he knows best. You may allow the successes and accomplishments that the enemy has provided to him and corrupt them in his mind as his own achievements. You are capable of having him believe that the struggles he was facing as a young man and the direct and indisputable guidance his stubborn and confused creator provided to him during his times of need were in fact his own ideas. Place the seedlings of thought that where he stands now in life, full of distinguished accomplishment and success, was due to his own greatness and capacity.

If you successfully align him with these thoughts and ideas, we have experienced a positive reaction from the enemy, whereby, for reasons we do not understand, he begins to take away the blessings and restrict success from individuals. This may take many forms. It could be financial where his earthly wealth is greatly reduced, social when he begins to lose friends and other people he has cared about, who leave him due to the changed and unattractive person he may be becoming or it may be physical with his health falling under attack.

Whatever the reason, whatever the cause, you must ensure that he focuses on the negative aspects of his embarrassing fall from superiority. Open up old wounds of insecurities and fear of failure, and let him feel the heat of his pathetic failures. It will be a good time for you and I encourage you to savour the sweet tones of his mournful cries for whatever he has lost. There is a warning to heed in this time of crisis. Some humans have been shown to develop unexpected attributes of humility and understanding during falls such as what I have described. It is absolutely imperative that instead of seeing lessons from the experience, he remains focused on the emotional turmoil of what he has experienced and relies solely on his ego to have him attempt to claw back to his previous position in society.

I will not tell you the number of individuals who have escaped our grasp when they were so well amongst our ranks just because they decided that because they had lost so much they had nothing to lose and therefore could reignite a relationship with the Enemy. It is completely counterintuitive and our best scholars are still attempting to understand what the relationship is between failure and a spontaneous loving relationship with those irritating lovers of light. Do they not understand that retribution and justice is due to all of the shriveling humans, best served hot in our ever frothing chambers of fire? In other news, we have recently received word that we will need to commence rationing and the stores of souls fall ever lower. Our father recently held a banquet in order to mark 70 years since the collection of one of the leaders of the second world war. I've heard that his soul, black and rich in flavour, is now only able to be enjoyed by senior ranks. This is why your work is so important. This is why you must not fail in acquiring this soul.

Yours with affection,

Maniacus

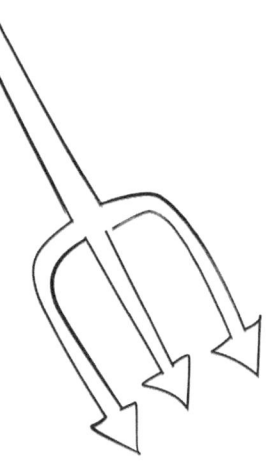

CLOSE TO DEATH

My Dearest Incendus,

This is it. This is your last chance. He lies on our friend, death's bed. You have much to do and little time to do it. As any human can be, being in a position of vulnerability causes a number of chain reactions. Firstly, you are primed to insert the fear of death into his heart. Since the days of his forefathers and mothers, this has been all too easy to do, due to its unnatural existence. Yes, the son has removed it as an absolute from their lives, but in moments where the passing of a soul from the physical into the spiritual is at hand, they all too easily forget. This is why you must consistently overload his thoughts and emotions with the deep and blackened associated fears of dying:

- Fear
- Anger
- Regret
- Resentments

Of course, you are to expect the enemy will be hard at work also, attempting to calm his mind, body and spirit and prepare him for departure. I cannot express the importance of providing any last-ditch efforts to convince him that the enemy is not his Lord and Saviour and that he should rather focus on the earthly pursuits of medicine, a fear of death and a perpetual regret for all the things he did not do in his life. It is possible that he will experience the greatest levels of fear he has ever known during this critical time and it is your responsibility to guide and grow it to allow the great black beast of the abyss to fester in the potential glee that your patients may be yours in a few hours.

You will also find in the weeks, days and hours leading up to the passing of your patient that you have unusual access to certain components of his emotions, whilst restrictions in areas that you have always had up until this point. This is to be expected as various extreme psychological phenomena are at play as they come to terms with their impending bodily death. It is for this reason that you must employ ingenuity and proactivity in designing impromptu mechanisms of infiltrating both the thought processes and emotional state of the boy.

Consider not knowing the future Incendus. I suppose we can in some way empathise in that we do not know when the enemy will charge, in what they call the Second Coming. However, imagine being in the position of a weak and insignificant human, about to pass into an apparent, without knowing for certain what occurs the moment the light fades from their eyes. It is not so much the fear of death that you should be focusing on but rather fear of the unknown. This fear is relevant to all humans, not just atheists. In the case of your Christian patient, you're able to question if he was a good enough human to enter the kingdom of our sworn enemy. Suggest that he did not lead a life wholesome enough, selfless enough or kind enough. Most importantly, have him forget that the only requirement for him to enter the brilliant gates of light in the ethereum above is to acknowledge the son of God, Lord and Saviour and that his sins are forgiven.

This is what everything boils down to. This simple concept cannot be accepted, believed in and glorified at the moment of his last breath and final heartbeat. I trust he is in pain, aided by your brothers? Have this cloud and confuse his mind. Make room for him to generate one final resentment towards the Creator.

Hopefully if he is conscious and sentient, have him look upon his wife, children, grandchildren and great-grandchildren with great sadness and longing, with a desire to remain alive for just a little bit longer, wanting to gaze into the eyes of his loved ones. Consume his mind with worldly concepts and earthly concerns as opposed to the Peace that the Creator promises for a Christian such as he. Unfortunately for you, he has lived a full life and given much good to the world, so there is little for you to negotiate in contorting his actions into some form of spiritual regret. Have him concerned about his responsibilities, for example caring for his wife who he does not want to leave to become a widow. Is he questioning the medication he is receiving from other professionals who are caring for his health? Is he uncomfortable or experiencing something that is shameful or embarrassing? These are all elements that you were able to exacerbate and exaggerate during your final battle.

I warn you Incendus. Although your reports show that he is apparently on a positive trajectory to enter our Territory very soon, I do want to ensure you are completely and transparently aware of what is at stake. His soul will be consumed or you will be consumed in its place, for all time. I would like to say thank you for your continued efforts to seek advice and wisdom from me, your esteemed Demon Excelsior and that you have carried out your task with ambition and with a ruthlessness that the job of Temptation requires. I trust you will experience the great satisfaction pulling the soul from the wasted Embers of the body and dragging him down to the great tunnels of the Earth and Stone to the warm bosom of our great leaders' homes. Either way I will see you soon.

Yours with great affection and expectation,

Maniacus

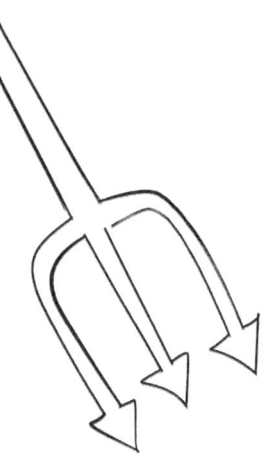

AFTER DEATH

To Insignificant Incendus,

Oh you horrid, floundering fool.

You have failed your assignment and you are to blame.

The light of the enemy has outshone you and all is lost, for you at least. I should have known this was an inevitable outcome from the very beginning.

I must say Incendus, I took particular delight in your slobbering mess of an imploration in your previous letter. You truly believe that my niceties of correspondence past were sourced in sincerity. Such an error only confirms your gross and undeniable confusion as to our nature.

Do not seek ANY pity or worse, mercy, from me. This is intrinsically an abstraction of the enemy, and I won't engage in such heresy. You cretin. You hilariously inadequate, incompetant imbecile. I revel in your fear and desperation and become drunk on the drink of your anguish. Consider what you have asked of me and compare it to what the humans ask of their Creator. There is no difference. And I feel justified that you will never again disgrace our kind again by allowing a much needed soul to wander out of our grasp.

You are due for the perpetually persistent and eternal hand of justice and as I hope you quiver in your shrivelled skin as you accept what lies in store for you. You know all too well what a ravenous breed we are. In taking the place of your would be, should be condemned human's soul, we will have to feed off your morsel of an essence. Let me be clear, you are in no way a substitute for the sweet nodes of tender good intentions or the delectable blind eye atrocities that we should have been enjoying. No, you do not nearly present yourself as a satisfying meal, yet this is the law. We will have to endure the less than satisfying pieces of your bitter insolence and undignified existence.

You have allowed a soul, precious in its capacity for corruption, to be made incorruptible by our baffling enemy. The excruciating brightness and deafening noise that you would have experienced at the moment of your assignment's passing was the arrival of the enemy, prepared to escort the "saved" individual to his new place of rest and perpetual joy. We have no concept of what this means for your lost human, other than the undeniable fact that as a direct result of the creator's son's actions all those centuries ago, we cannot touch him. Within the rites of the universal laws of nature, his debt is repaid and he is free from our bonds. In the name of the son, he is unshackled and stripped of all sin. That name that we cannot even utter, of a God and a man who committed acts we do not understand. It is an abomination to see such events occur, and I hope the shame of the moment is infecting your entire being. I can only imagine the powerlessness you would have demonstrated as you were ripped and stripped from his essence. And now you are returning home... empty handed.

You allowed your soul to experience the natural restoration of its place amongst his master, his own creator, of whose image he was created. And of course, at the moment of his passing, he saw you and all the ways you have mounted an attack on his eternal life. I'm sure you felt naked, exposed and ashamed while he was taken by the loving and welcoming hands of the enemy's leader. Not that you would've seen what he looks like. We simply cannot be in his presence. As a demon with an impeccable field record, I have never personally experienced the described burn that our kind experienced in the presence of the holy enemy. I just hope you were wailing as our condemned do.

I do not know whether it was your stupidity or shortsightedness, or if it was simply bad luck, you know full well the outcome is the same for you. As you are dragged back home by your once colleagues and friends, enjoy the final moments of your trivial existence as an entity not being consumed. In the meantime, think of your soul, safe and happy in the presence of this almighty. I will see (and taste) you soon.

Yours with hungry affection,

Maniacus

LETTER FROM THE HUMAN TO HIS WIFE ON THEIR WEDDING DAY

My my moonlit muse,

For the first time in my life, I just don't have the words. I have only everything to feel. But this is a letter, so I am left to at least try and express myself.

My darling, sweet sweet girl. Today is the day we have worked towards, fought for, anguished over and looked forward to for so very long. Our day has just begun, and who knows how the next 20 hours or so are going to transpire, but I am certain of at least one undeniable truth. As we go about the hurricane of activities, ceremonies, duties and formalities, my mind is only thinking of you, and my unquenchable thirst to bring you every happiness and joy that this world can offer. As God as my witness and third partner in this relationship, I vow to treasure our unity with my entire being. I will continue to unceasingly look for opportunities to embed joy, enthusiasm, energy and passionate love into our marriage, because God I simply cannot resist doing anything else.

I want to make you laugh. Always and forever.

I promise to support you in every one of your ventures, whether they be professional, personal, emotional or spiritual. Even if I don't understand why, I will be there, with a banner, probably some face paint... pom poms and a music video will definitely be involved, and you will only receive cries of encouragement and motivation from me while I film every moment. It'll be embarrassing for you. Sorry.

I want to thank you for your countless sacrifices and for your relentless capacity to help me in every hour of my needs. You are brave, thoughtful and selfless, and I will try to emulate these virtues every day.

We are taking a leap of faith together, and there is absolutely no one else on this Earth that I would want to be jumping with.

As I take your hand and you take my name,
I love you eternal. This, I proclaim.

Now go put on that dress, and I'll see you at the altar. DON'T BE LATE.

Let's get married!

For the last time in my life,

Your violently happy attacked fiance.

www.ingramcontent.com/pod-product-compliance
Lightning Source LLC
Chambersburg PA
CBHW020020030726
47499CB00007B/2202